*W*eregirls

Birth of the Pack

$\mathcal{W}$eregirls

Birth of the Pack

Petru Popescu

A TOM DOHERTY
ASSOCIATES BOOK
TOR® NEW YORK

WEREGIRLS: BIRTH OF THE PACK

Copyright © 2007 by Petru Popescu

Book design by Mary A. Wirth

A Tor Teen Book
Published by Tom Doherty Associates, LLC
175 Fifth Avenue
New York, NY 10010

www.tor.com

Tor® is a registered trademark of Tom Doherty Associates, LLC.

Library of Congress Cataloging-in-Publication Data

Popescu, Petru, 1944–
    Weregirls : birth of the pack / Petru Popescu.—1st ed.
        p. cm.
    "A Tom Doherty Associates book."
    Summary: When sixteen-year-old Lily and her friends Nikki, Arielle, and
Grazia start up a girls' soccer club at their South Pasadena high school and name
their team the Weregirls, they soon discover some unusual things about themselves as they become drawn into the age-old struggle between good and evil.
    ISBN-13: 978-0-7653-1641-7
    ISBN-10: 0-7653-1641-2
    [1. Supernatural—Fiction. 2. Soccer—Fiction. 3. High schools—Fic-
tion. 4. Schools—Fiction.] I. Title.
    PZ7.P7942Wer   2007
    [Fic]—dc22

                                                                    2007013216

First Edition: September 2007

Printed in the United States of America

0 9 8 7 6 5 4 3 2 1

*To Chloe, my inspiration for this series,
and to Adam and Iris*

And I must borrow every changing shape
To find expression . . .

—T. S. ELIOT, "Portrait of a Lady"

PART ONE

Captain's Log

1

September

This was the open letter for our school paper, the *Highlights*. I wrote it all myself. But I thought, hey, I shouldn't be narcissistic, so I let Nikki, Arielle, and Grazia cosign it. The four of us started playing soccer on our street when we were seven. And my dad was our first coach. He also nicknamed us the Weregirls, the meaning of which I'll explain presently. But first, the letter:

*To our whole girl population, grades 9–12:
What about starting some association football,
commonly known as soccer in America, at
South Pas? So that we girls can excel at a team
sport, which, by the way, originated in the*

mists of prehistory—Inca Indians kicked balls of llama skin in the courtyards of Machu Picchu, and the Roman legionnaires played a ball game with offense and defense. So why shouldn't we have the same kind of opportunity? Other high schools, like in L.A., already have girls' soccer teams! Friends, think about it. Even if the equality tip doesn't move you, think about the workout. In just a few weeks, you'll look sculpted. *Not to speak of the pure pleasure of the game. We'll play to kick, to knock shoulders, to head-butt the ball, to* shout. *Major release! That's the message from the four of us. We're hereby requesting the school authorities to bless this new club, which we're naming the Weregirls, and every female student 9th to 12th grade is invited to join, irregardless* (Mr. Harris, the journalism teacher, says "irregardless" is a "nonstandard word." I find it really expressive. He also says that I tend to write "screaming journalism"! Whatever!) *of creed, race, or the physical shape you're in. See you on the field, Weregirls!*

Signed: Lily Willison
(I did give myself first credit),
Nikki Stone, Arielle Knelling, Grazia Barbieri

So, our proposal for a girls' soccer team gets published in the school newspaper. The school doesn't say no, doesn't say yes right away either. Coach Brum, the boys' coach, shrugs. "Chicks' football, huh? Might be cute to watch, but . . . hmm . . ." I spared him a speech on his sexism (chicks! cute!). Coach Brum wears baggy pants and his shirt out, trying to seem hip; he manages to look old and depressed, his youth passed him by, now *we* pass him by! I ask for support from Ms. Padgett, woman and principal. She nods thoughtfully. "Girls' soccer, that sounds doable. I'll have to talk it over with the athletic director. Did you mention this to your mom, Lily?"

I remember this in such detail. What the others said. What I said. "Of course," I hurry to reply. "My mom thinks it's a great idea."

"I'm so glad she does," Ms. Padgett says. (Why my mom is referred to as such a trusted authority, I'll enlighten the readers soon.)

So, Ms. Padgett confers with Coach Brum, who's also the athletic director, and with some other teachers, then gets back to me and tells me, due to budget restrictions the school can't sanction us as an official team. But we could start a girls' soccer club. "Like the chess club. They're not an official school team, but they have matches with other school clubs in the area." I don't even know who's in the chess club—geeks with glasses sniffling over a board game? I don't care. Official, unofficial, we're going to have a team and play!

Ms. Padgett is really not so uncool about it. She tells Coach Brum to find us a place to play. Brum invites me to go with him to the running track adjoining the school, to measure if it could fit a soccer field. Inside the track there is a rectangle of sun-bleached grass two hundred feet long and about eighty feet wide. A soccer field, by all standards. All we have to do is draw the touchlines, and build the gates.

"You can train here," Brum says, "and invite other teams playing in the area . . . if there are any. Now, soccer's not as tough as football, but it's still a lot of scrimming and scrumming. . . . You sure you girls will like that?"

"Girls can be pretty tough," I reply with an undercurrent of menace, which he misses. "And we love running."

"Running! Ha!" He burps nostalgically, shifts his feet on the grass. "All right. You're in command, Lily." One hour later, Brum hands me a copy of the key to the steel padlock that seals off the running track.

So now I'm free to organize games and training sessions! Even in the evenings up to 9 P.M., if I notify him, and if I present a register book to the night guard (who snoozes off in a completely different building) in which I sign us in and out.

I've never been a straight-A student, though I do have good vocab—and I never felt super civic about school, but when I get that key in my palm, I feel a rush of pride. Kids should be told to create new things at their schools; I don't know why that's not done more often. It can't be the kids—we're so willing. Anyway, now I'm officially the club founder and first captain of my team!

That night, after receiving the key to the track, I started jotting the events in a little log book. I'm aware of my historical responsibilities as founder and recorder—and I won't drop this, as I did with my earlier journals. Of course, I could write a real diary, but that requires discipline, while if I do it only when the events dictate, it's more suspenseful. And I abbreviate words in my own way, so they're really hrdtfgr by someone else peeping in.

(Hrdtfgr equals hard to figure, hmm. Not so hard really, I'll make it harder.)

In the next few weeks, me, Grazia, Nikki, and Arielle did everything. We bought the paint to draw the touchlines, and asked my mom to ask the police department to lend us a line-tracing vehicle. There is such a thing. It's responsible for signs painted on the drivable parts of roadways or in parking lots. Our school has one too, in fact, but since we're not an official team, wouldn't you know it, we couldn't use the school's equipment! But the po said yes and sent theirs over, for one afternoon, complete with a driver. We built the goals ourselves, from scratch. We launched a public subscription in the school paper, for money to buy lumber, and didn't raise enough. But after cannibalizing a tree house that a classmate of ours had outgrown, and after countless splintered fingers, we built the goals, and started scrimmage after school. Kids came and plopped down on the ground and watched and yelled, and after the game threw us kudos, like, "Hey, black tee (me), you the team captain? What's your name?" or, "You, the redhead chick (Arielle)! You kick so nasty, I feel it!"

We played by the most basic rules at first, almost never with full teams. Eight of the original players, after hits with the ball in the nose, mashed toes, kicks in the gut, accidental or not so accidental, quit. But another twenty signed up—these girls really want to get *sculpted*! So in these past three weeks, our ragtag team, no rule book, no real coach (I'm coach *and* captain), in our own shorts, T-shirts, and sneakers reinforced with tape, played "informals" with teams from Azusa, Ontario, Crestmore, Mentone, Upper West Highlands. Real ratty holes. There's this underground soccer circuit of mostly Latin kids (and even some Indians), who play soccer because it's the prime sport in Mexico. Parents of such kids write soccer meet schedules in ballpoint pen on any kind of paper, tacking them by the cash register of the neighborhood taqueria: *Domingo, fútbol a la 5 P.M.* We played against Latin boys from migrant families, on unlevel fields with not-by-code goalposts, with twenty volunteer refs shouting in Spanish, and a barbecue flaming on right by. Hot dogs for all.

The Latin boys were blown away when this horde of gringas with ponytails dropped on them out of an old bus that Nikki's uncle, a retired car mechanic, reanimated. He's driving us personally to our out-of-town games. The Latin boys would've never played their own girls—they made that clear. But we were a curiosity they couldn't pass up!

They played rough, but kind of gave us the games at the start, and even told us we'd be welcome again—if we kept it on the DL. Because their families are illegal. Now, that's way down DL! And I who thought Mom would eventually drive us to the games! Not if we played illegals; if they glimpsed Mom, they'd scatter like birds from buckshot—Mom's a cop and always in blue. That's why she's treated like such an authority . . . mom and cop, double the power. But really she couldn't, because of her work hours. With soccer itself, Mom was kind of okay. Like, "Lily, I'm glad that you're playing, but you're getting bruised all over. Isn't that game too aggressive for you?" That was funny, I swear! "And you're tearing up a T-shirt every week!"

"Yeah, and I need some nice T-shirts. I don't want to wear trash anymore!"

"You never called what I bought you trash before!"

"Maybe it wasn't trash for the ninth grade. Mom, please, can you give me and the girls a ride to L.A.? To Santee Alley downtown? They got True Religion knockoffs."

"Right now?"

"Why not?"

Mom strapped on her bulletproof vest. "I can't now. I'll be late for overtime."

She works overtime, *always,* so we can save for my college tuition. Last night, she was on regular patrol, and now she's rushing off to overtime. "Also, that Santee stuff is stitched by kids in Bangladesh for two cents a day."

"Mom, how else will kids in Bangladesh gain exposure to high-end fashions? Anyway, me and the girls know *exactly* where those knockoffs are. We'll be in and out, and it's not like you have to pay for the gas to get us there, since you're a cop. If you need an excuse to be there, walk down the block and arrest someone while we try on our knockoffs."

Can you believe this *contention,* for some lousy knockoffs? Instead of loading us into the patrol car pronto, storming downtown with sirens blaring, so we could be done shopping quicker?

But with Mom, no is no. So I escalated. "I have *no* clothes, and we need some better money than what you're making, if I'm to keep going to this school filled with richie-rich brats, and drive a car that even compares to their cars—and stop making me feel like I'm a vacuous ditz!"

She escalated too. "Stop making me feel like I'm a bad mother."

"If you were a good mother you would've driven me there already!" (I felt my cell phone in my pocket, throbbing with calls from the Were-girls: Hey, are we going shopping, or what?)

"Lily, I can't do things like that. It's my job."

"Oh God! Dad wouldn't have said no!" Then I see that I almost made her cry, so *I* cry. I too have a heart, you know? And she did take us downtown—the following Sunday, on the metro-rail. And I got in trouble again, because I found some great knee-high team socks, and Grazia, who always has cash (she takes it direct from her dad's pizzeria till), offered to buy me a pair, which I deserved—I'm the OWG (original Weregirl), the founding vixen. But Mom wouldn't have that. She bought me the pair herself, and said from now on soccer was on a budget.

So I hate Mom.

Okay, okay, I love her too.

It's all pretty complicated, because Mom recently discovered this fellow patrolman, Tim. So she's too busy to supervise me like she did before, which is very cool, but the guy's at our house all the time—not so cool. Anyway, now I spend more time at school than at home due to soccer practice. Nikki's uncle plus some deadbeat divorce dads happy to share *any time* with their twice-a-month daughters keep driving us to our eccentric little games, and I'm a talked-about kid because I started this. I've never done anything before that I could consider a personal achievement. So I should be totally happy.

I am and I'm not, because I don't like my body all of a sudden. I have this gut, not so big that you'd spot it through my clothes, but it drives me crazy, and it grew muscular and hard as I kept stopping balls with it. My feet are bumpy and rather large, not boy feet, but almost, and after a game my toes are purple. My face is okay, but my chin's too small, and my mouth—I can't decide, is my mouth too big, or a little too small? I can't even complain about all this, because Mom's like, "Lily, you look *fine!*" *always.* But Mom has an agenda: Mom thinks if I'm not gorgeous, I won't have sex early.

She can chill. I'm not gorgeous.

Anyway, lo and behold, the *Daily South Pasadenan* (the "official rag," as we who put out the *Highlights* call the grown-up local paper) printed a story about our team getting ready for our first home game. I was in two practice photos, kicking, my hair out of its ponytail, really billowing—wish I had my dad's hair, black and straight and full of body, but I got Mom's, a lazy light brown, just okay. Soccer helps—when my hair gets dusty, it stiffens it. The best line in that story was what *I* said: "We're a testament to young women everywhere, and really want to make waves in the community!"

They quoted Principal Padgett too, saying she was proud of us and knew we would be a success. The school paper reprinted the story and conducted an interview among the students, who were asked what they thought of soccer and were they proud of our team. They published a lot of the replies. Many boys said they hadn't thought we could pull it off, and Lily Willison was a better organizer than she seemed, but generally they were supportive.

That same day, in the *Pasadenan*'s business section (which is a skimpy two pages), it was announced that our city had just gone from bankrupt back to solvent, due to a loan arranged by a certain Howard Hewlit, a native South Pasadenan who had returned to live here, after years in New York, with his whole family, which includes a daughter my age. Howard Hewlit owns real estate, and businesses and hotels all around Pasadena, and I heard Mr. Harris, our journalism teacher, mumble, "He was chased out of New York for..." I think he said "insider trading," but I wasn't really listening. "Now he wants to play hero back home. He's putting his daughter in our school." Harris is bitter— he was once the editor who made the *Pasadenan* into a real paper, then he disagreed with some policy and had to quit.

Andra Hewlit in our school—that felt made up. With their kind of money she should be in Switzerland someplace. I didn't even think about it. We'd gotten so popular all of a sudden, we couldn't walk the halls without turning heads—so who cared about some new rich girl? Then, two days ago, after practice, as we peeled off our slushy socks, Grazia said, "Maybe Andra will join our team and her dad will buy us a new ball, or new outfits or something. Why don't you write her a friendly note, Lily?"

"Huh?" I said. "When'd she make it over here?"

"You're full of it," Grazia said. "Weren't you with me this morning, when she came to school, in a Jag?" I narrowed my eyes like I connected. Oh, *that* Andra. I still acted like she was a fly on a sock. Grazia continued. "Maybe we could get her email address." Nikki started looking at me, and I knew that she could sense my resistance. "Write her a note, and stick it on the intra-student notice board," Nikki said, and then waited, and I said nothing.

Nikki's my best friend. Well, they all are. We grew up together, all four. But I'm closest with Nikki. Nikki's short, but she's a fierce offense. She wears hoops, one in her nose. She's cute and the fastest runner on our team. Grazia is round, with nice olive skin and wavy brown hair, like an old Italian painting. I'm glad she's big, she's our goalie, more body to stop the ball—*thud! thunk!*—that's the ball in play, zapping into Grazia. Our fans are not nice to her. "Come on, Grazia, shake those pizza pies!" they shout. Her dad owns the best pizzeria in South Pas. Arielle is long-limbed, with brassy red hair and a good face; she's pretty. She's kind of an airhead, but I still like her. My friends have character. Definitely.

Now, none of us are rich. Grazia always has

cash, but she's not like *diseased* from it; she still has a lovable innocence, always ready for pack fun. Arielle's competitive—her mom's this attorney who passed her bar pregnant with her, and now she wants Arielle's dad to make some real money—he's a court reporter, but you can't make anything off that today. All true crime is invented. So Arielle's dad is depressed. Nikki became an orphan at ten. Her parents died in a car crash—now she lives with that uncle who's driving us to our games, and his wife; they already raised a set of kids. He saves his juice for driving us; she doesn't even make it to open school night. Nikki's free, but she lives with two ghosts, and she's poor. Anyway, America's wealth is supposed to be shrinking, but where is it shrinking? I look on TV, all I see is rich-rich. That's why I don't watch too much TV; it's real pressure on someone like me.

"I don't want to write to Andra," I growled. "There's something in the way everyone talks about her that gives me the creeps. I know I'm not jealous, guaranteed. What's she got to make me jealous?"

"Come on, Cap," Nikki said. "We've got to be political."

"All right. You write the note. I'll sign it."

So later that night, Nikki wrote a note inviting Andra to watch us scrimmage, and maybe play with us, see if she likes it. I signed it. It got tacked on the intra-student notice board.

Next day, it's still pinned on the board. No reply.

The next day, and the next day, and the next day, it's still pinned on the board. Then it vanishes. It fell off, or someone took it down.

I stop checking the board for a reply—she probably never read my note. But I'm not going to write another one. I don't care.

2

Today, we had our best practice yet! Our team's shaping up. Afterward, Nikki threw her arm over my shoulder and told me that my dad would've been proud.

Yeah. I wish Dad could see us.

Dad was the one who first played soccer with us. He bought us our first ball, and taught us how to dribble, veering his big body this way, that way, jumping aside so as not to land his big police shoes on our little feet—then he'd take off his shoes and socks, turn up his pant cuffs, and train us barefoot. Never getting his toes bruised. Amazing. He soothed our tears when we got hit in the face by the ball. He ran alongside, his breath intercut by kicks and counter-kicks. "Look how easy it comes, Lily. . . . This is the most natural game. . . . Kick a pebble or a bag of Fritos, if it starts rolling, don't you wish you could kick it forever?"

Yeah. A ball to kick is a kids' most wondrous toy. Hard, but responsive. Live at the slightest touch. Kick it right, it shoots like a well-aimed asteroid! Into the net! *Whizz-zap!* Yeaaahhh!

Dad used to buy us pizza at Grazia's dad's place, after me and my girlfriends played. We brought it home to eat and he told us stories about famous games and players. About who started kickball as an organized sport in America: the American Indians, of course. "Cheyenne girls on reservations still play kickball today." I can see my dad just now, sitting at our kitchen table overflowing with ravaged pizza boxes.

"The girls, not the boys?" Grazia asked, her caramel-colored eyes focused on my dad.

"In some tribes, it's exclusively a girls' game," he said. "Indian girls dribble, kick the ball up in the air, and count how many times they can kick it. They do it ten times easy, before it falls down again."

Ten! I could do it four, tops, before losing my balance, or the ball.

"Who taught the Indians how to play ball?" I asked, though I already knew the answer.

"The weregirls," said my dad. "In the beginning of the world, the weregirls, who were magical animals, lived on Earth, but the Earth was cold and unfriendly, because there was no sun in the sky to warm it up. The weregirls were miserable from the cold, so they all got together, raised their muzzles toward the sky like the wolves do, and howled like the wolves. Out of the warmth of their breaths came this fiery ball, the sun, which soared up into the sky.

"So the sky warmed up the Earth for the first time. The weregirls stopped shivering from the cold, and were so happy and joyful, they ran around yelping and snipping each other, like pretty pups."

Me and my friends were seven, or nine, or ten back then, and hadn't believed in Santa Claus for a while, but we loved the magical stories that my dad was such a master at telling. We imagined the magical pups, so joyful after having warmed up the Earth.

"Then," said my dad, "everything on Earth became green and fruitful, and lots of other breeds were born. Then one breed of evil creatures arose. They slaughtered other creatures and ate them, polluted the air and knocked down the sacred trees that the weregirls worshipped. They were really trying to force the weregirls off the planet. But then the whole breath of life rose against that breed of evil creatures, and called the supreme goddess Hopi, whose name means "the peaceful one." Hopi heard life's complaint, and bounced down from her throne in heaven to rescue the weregirls. With Hopi's help, they pummeled the breed, and locked them up inside the ridges and peaks of the Earth's mountain ranges. Then Hopi figured she should create some creatures who would always be in alliance with the weregirls. She thought about what they should be like and came up with the humans—a peaceful and loving species. The weregirls were happy, and the humans were happy. Those were the happiest days of life on Earth."

"But how did they start playing ball?" I asked again, though I knew the story by heart.

"They wanted to have some fun after doing such good for the Earth," said my dad. "So they got together again and put their little muzzles together, and blew out the moon, which they wanted to keep as a toy. The moon cooled off quickly, and the weregirls played ball with it. They bounced the moon with their noses, kicked it with fore and hind paws, dribbled it. . . . They've been playing ball with the moon ever since."

I was so proud of my dad's imagination. When my friends came to my house, Dad was the one who told us stories, which he made up. He hardly ever read to us out of a book.

"Why can't we see the weregirls play with the moon?" I asked.

"Because they play with it in the daytime," he said, "when we can't see the moon because of the sun glare. At night, they let the moon loose so it can be enjoyed by us, the humans. They're very nice and giving, the weregirls. Sometimes, during storms, the weregirls are playing soccer with the moon behind the clouds—when you hear claps of thunder, the weregirls are kicking and dribbling the moon."

Nikki said, "When my uncle took me to the zoo, the animals didn't play anything. They sat around bored and miserable."

"I'm not talking of animals in captivity. In freedom, any puppy plays with a ball. He sees it rolling, he jumps on it by instinct. In the desert, when coyotes corner an armadillo and it curls up, the coyotes roll it with their paws and nudge it with their noses. They want to eat it, but they love playing with the balled-up armadillo first. And if they get distracted by some other prey, they run off and give the armadillo a break."

"Weregirls are like wolf puppies, right?" Nikki asked.

"Yes, but larger, and prettier. They're not were-wolves." Dad laughed, guessing Nikki's next question. "That's Hollywood stuff. And there are no bad wolves either, not in Indian tales."

"Are you an Indian, Mr. Willison?" Arielle asked.

"Yes I am, honey. I worked patrol on an Indian reservation, and since I was a full-blood they let me watch the *minio mistai,* their secret dance about sacred animals, and ghosts and spirits."

My dad's parents lived on a reservation in Idaho. Since I could remember, they wrote us cards, inviting us to go up there for Thanksgiving, or for Christmas, but Mom kept finding reasons why we couldn't go. Mainly because of me—I was too little, I'd just had a tooth pulled, I was coming down with a cold—all excuses, I realized later. Mom didn't want me to get close to Dad's parents. And then, fate struck. My grandparents were in a truck with some other relatives, returning from a wedding. The truck overturned on an iced-up road. I didn't go to the funeral, nor did Mom. Dad alone went. When he came back, he told me that they had a tribal Indian burial, the real thing. I didn't care if Dad was an Indian or not. Dad was Dad. He didn't look very Indian, except his hair was so straight and hard. Both he and Mom wore their hair short, and acted enormously straight, because they were cops.

At the end of such an evening, the phone would ring. Dad would walk into the den, and pick up the phone there. But I could hear Mom's voice, clear and sharp, along with a police dispatcher's voice coming from her cruise car's radio.

"Matt? You took the girls home yet?"

"Just ready to drive them off," said Dad.

Mom got mad at him. "D'you know what time it is? They have school tomorrow."

"I know, Marcia. Easy shift tonight, hon?"

"Yep. No messy customers yet."

They talked like they ran a convenience store: tonight was her night at the cash register, tomorrow would be his night.

"Watch yourself. I love you," he said. I heard Mom reply, "Me too." Matter of fact, she was riding in the cruiser, with another cop next to her.

They hung up. Dad paced back from the den. "Let's clean up, weregirls," he said. "You do the table, and I'll do the sink." We whined. We were *sooo* exhausted. Dad started on the sink, quickly and efficiently, then helped us clean the kitchen table. Then he loaded us in his little Toyota, which he maintained with the same efficient care he put into everything—I snuggled next to him in front, and my friends piled up in back. We dropped them all off in under two minutes; we all lived in the same neighborhood.

Then we drove back home. I slipped into my pajamas, brushed my teeth, climbed into bed, said my prayers, and Dad came and tucked me in. He switched off the lights, and I asked him to sit by my bed. He told me not to worry about Mom being out on the beat. She was safe. The weregirls were protecting her; Dad had personally asked them to do so. I asked Dad if they protected him too, and he said he had one protection voucher from the weregirls and he'd given it to Mom. Because Mom was a female, and females aren't usually cops. But

Dad would be fine—he'd just been made a detective, no more 911 blue, as police uniforms were called in our house. He was less of a target.

"The weregirls are looking out for me anyway, because I'm their contact among the humans." He lowered his voice. "I'm the weregirls' undercover detective among the human breed."

I bolted up in bed and hugged him. "Are you, Dad? Are you?"

I loved his stories, with their fantastic, inconsistent logic. Consistent only in one respect: Dad was magical. He used his magic to protect Mom and me.

"We must do something nice for the weregirls," I said.

"I'm doing it already," he said. "That swimming pool I'm digging in the backyard—it's for them too. I'm going to put a shower next to the pool—late at night, the weregirls will run in sweaty after a game, and shower in our yard, and then swim. Weregirls love playing and then taking lots of showers, not like someone I know. . . ." He wagged his finger at me.

I whooped. "When are you finishing the pool, Daddy?"

He seemed slightly sad. "Soon, sweetie," he said.

As I fell asleep, my father's voice lullabied me, becoming distorted and dreamy. Belief and disbelief fought inside me, finally melting into one unflawed feeling: a happy childhood. . . .

In hindsight, I might've guessed that my parents were having problems, but they never fought— they "disagreed," was my father's way of putting it. That's how you measure the strength of love, he said, by overcoming disagreements.

I might've noticed that Mom and Dad never went out together anymore, or that when Dad came home, put on dirty clothes, and toiled at completing the pool, Mom went out to the pool with two mugs of coffee, but they didn't seem to enjoy that coffee. They talked in a way that sounded strained, and after such talks Dad worked poorly, which wasn't like him. . . . He finally put in that new shower, but not by the pool. He set it in the garage, against the back wall, and added a mirror and a sink. He bought a workbench and wood-carving tools, put them in the garage, and spent many hours there, explaining to me that undercover work was stressful, but that wood-carving helped him relax. When he returned late from work, he didn't come into the house but went to the garage and showered there. He said the shower by the master bedroom would wake up Mom.

But I was only seven, only eight, only ten, so I didn't understand. I didn't want to understand.

"Matt Willison, if you can hear me now, if you're driving that big black-and-white cruiser up along Heaven's freeways, remember us," was how Police Chief Noonan finished his eulogy for my dad. "Remember your brave loving wife. Your wonderful daughter. And us, your bereft colleagues. For we will always remember you. You're unforgettable and irreplaceable."

And then they lowered my dad into the dusty earth of a South Pas cemetery, and put a plaque on his tombstone mentioning that he was killed in the line of duty.

It's been five years.

Dad? From up along those heavenly freeways, can you see me now?

3

October, six weeks since we started the team

The weather's been passive-aggressive: rain, sun, fog, sun. But it's been good. We're learning to play, dribble, pass, connect as a team in any conditions. And we've got a boys' team coming to rematch us at home. From Sagemont, the rattiest hole we'd ever been to. A real desert ghetto.

We played at their field three weeks ago. Driving us there, Nikki's uncle told us how the U.S. government had contracted the village of Sagemont to service a toxic waste dump, back in the '50s. The people were given salaries and cheap housing for laying access roads and maintaining barbed wire fences. Then the dump was moved, but the people hung on. The rumor was that they were still paid by the government, to watch for strange growths in the desert.

As our van drove closer, we saw military-style houses set up in grids. The houses were old, some boarded up and condemned. Ghostly old cars and pickup trucks were left to waste on dusty front lawns. The place looked like it had been soaked in sludge, brown and burnt out; even the sky was creepy, clouds clogged up with the threat of rain, yet they didn't release one drop of water. In the shadow of a gas station, a weird, mutated invasion of bugs lay crushed by tires. Then . . .

On the soccer field, more dust than grass, we faced the Sagemont boys: cute, tanned raw, and kicking like cannons. We were so stoked to play, we didn't care. But the Sagemont boys played so savage, our first opponents who wouldn't give us a point. They beat us. We got back on our bus, all sweaty, didn't even say ten words to them, or them to us.

Two weeks later, they come to South Pas. Rematch. And the sun's back too. In fact it gets hot like summer, blistering a sky without a cloud.

We have our biggest turnout of fans yet. We have no bleachers—just a few benches, and the grass. Kids kick back on their rears and elbows. They heckle the Sagemont boys when they stumble from their bus. To us, they yell, "Hey, Were-girls! Nasty all the way!"

"You got it!" my girls shout back.

Meanwhile—the cap sets the tone—I stride out in welcome, shake hands with their cap, then point to where we set up a little hospitality table for the guests: bottled waters, Fritos, two baskets of oranges. Paid from our own pockets, of course. I even stationed two fans to chase off our boys if they try to raid the bottled water—they can use the school fountains.

I'm happy.

And we score the first goal! When Nikki has a breakaway, their goalie comes out to challenge her, too early. Nikki flicks it over his head, into the net. South Pas goes ape. The Sagemont boys are stunned we've gotten better. They swear between their teeth, get physical. But we score again. Yeah! We get so confident, we size up the boys who play our positions. Nikki's and Arielle's are ugly, and mash them. Their center mid, my position, is cute though. Tall, with brown hair, and big hands. Checks me as he steals my ball—he's smart! Smiles as we knock into each other. He wasn't there the other game, I would remember. His team calls at him: "Josh! Go, Josh!"

We fight midfield. Good legs on him. I sort of bump his butt. Rock-hard.

"You're aggressive," he pants to me.

"Shut up," I pant in reply.

He gets quiet, concentrates. I do too. I don't look at him anymore, I'm here to play, right? They score. Boom! From him passing the ball. I get angry, really bump him. He gets away, passes the ball, they score again. Dirt covers Grazia from head to toe. She dives to catch this last one, nothing doing. That Josh kid, he's the soul of their team.

At halftime, we huddle to strategize. But I realize *they* don't have a strategy; they're these young animals, run so fast, shoot so hard, they have us by energy alone. When they bump us, we fly aside. After this, they'll go back to their hole. Only Josh has a kind of gentlemanly grace; he smiles when he's faster than me, like, *Hey, don't get upset. It's just a game!*

Arielle and Nikki can't wait for it to end. Nikki says, "If I rub with my pimply goon one more time, I'll hurl on the field. Lily, let's switch."

Arielle gasps, "Yeah, she's got the only cute one—don't hoard him, Lily."

"I'm not hoarding him. He's a sweaty mess."

"I saw him smile at you," says Arielle. "At least if we lose, maybe you'll hook up before they leave."

"Me?" I'm outraged. "He's a lump, and we'll win. Nikki, you play him."

"Cool." Nikki spits on the grass. She glares at Josh. "You're mine, baby."

Just then, he runs to his position, sees that I moved, looks over at me, and smiles again. Maybe he's not smiling at me specifically. But he smiles. Like he's saying, *I'm not a danger to a girl. On the field, or after.* Now, a guy can always be a danger to a girl, but you never know it till you meet that guy up close, and that's the problem with being a female. So when a guy throws smiles, girls become so open to it, it's pathetic. Josh wipes his arm over his sweaty face, our fans yell, fresh sweat pours out on earlier sweat, the game's on, we might still win. Josh smiles! I smile back. I can't help it.

So we go into the second half. Grazia makes a diving save, throws an outlet pass to Arielle, who turns, beats the tall lanky boy she defends, kicks it to me. I take the pass, loft it high, over to Nikki. Nikki, who's so much smaller than Josh, slips under his armpit practically, back to me. I kick, I score! It feels so great, to see Josh stunned! All at once, I know: after the game, we'll talk. It feels so certain, I'm a little dazed. We jog back on defense, the ball rolls to me, I hear the hopeful gasp of the crowd, then a mocking voice: "Don't mess up, Weregirl!" The voice laughs out that last word. "Weregirl."

I look off to where the school lies sprawled out on the grass and see a blond girl. Standing up, in a denim miniskirt and boots that look expensive even at that distance, she stares at me with arms folded. Her hair's so blond against the background grass, it glows, neonlike. Even with sunshine pouring down on her head! I try to kick, and whiff. What a jinxer, that girl. . . . Josh gets the ball.

"Kick it, Josh!" she shouts. Weird, how she calls his name, but his team's been yelling it.

Josh scores.

"Nice, Josh!" she shouts, and flourishes her arm at him.

Yeah, now I know who she is: Andra Hewlit. Two other girls who go to South Pas, both of them blond, and always dressed up—we call them the Barbies—stand on each side of Andra, a half step aside, as if to mark her importance. Andra has blue eyes—usually, light-colored eyes don't register so strong at a distance. But hers do. With a kind of cheerful hardness in them, a confidence that feels too consistent, strange. She turns and walks away, as if the game was played, and Nikki spits at me, "Come on, Cap, get your head back on! They're kicking our butts!"

I wipe the sweat off my face, angry. "Let's switch back," I throw at Nikki. Done, and when Josh dribbles by, I shoulder him so hard, he loses his balance. Our team takes the ball. "Hey, what'd I do?" He laughs as he springs back next to me. And he shoulders me back, boom! I fly aside— even my teeth rattle, and he springs away, then peeks back, am I okay? I wince and run up and neither of us push anymore. He plays well.

We lose.

We gather ourselves. Our guys break onto the field, loudly supportive: "Hey, good game, they're not better than you—but how'd you whiff that ball, Lily, you tripped?" Sullen, I gather my hair, rub my shoulder. The Sagemonters grab the last water bottles and troop away toward their bus. Josh turns, stares at me, our eyes totally lock. Then, I hear Andra's voice. The same hard cheerfulness. "You guys have speed. If you had a decent coach . . ." I'm behind Josh; his teammates make room for him. Andra stands by the bus, boots and all; our guests, still steaming energy, ring her in. So she takes a half step back, lays her hand, very nice nails, on the side of the bus.

"Here's Lily," she says, laughing. "She put this club team together, no real training, no coach . . . but she's magical!"

I size her up—like, I need her to tell me I'm good? She's not very tall—her boots help—but she's so pretty. Fairest hair, naturally wavy, blue eyes, very clear, even their hardness is becoming. A turned-up nose, just the right size. She looks like she never had a pimple. Super-cliché? Maybe, but I grieve that I'm not like her. My fans are staring at her—gentlemen prefer blondes, last century, this century, always.

"You still did good, Weregirl!"

Then she turns to Josh. "How come you're not the cap?" Josh shrugs, while the guy I shook hands with is standing right there, hearing this. "You're the best one, Josh," she adds, then sweeps her blue eyes at our dusty field. "Too bad we don't have a decent facility, so you guys could've showered too, like after a real game. I played back east. I know Ed Sloan, the guy who runs the Junior National League, I could tell him about you, Josh."

Josh is quiet. The whole crowd—them, us—is quiet. This TV ad got off the screen and walked down here, and now she's cramming her message in every word she says: power. Then she glances at me. Behind all that trumpeting, I sense curiosity, maybe also . . . she wants something? I stare back, surly: *What, you never met my type? This is me, thanks. Cop's daughter.* Because I sense it immediately: if Josh wanted to talk to me before this, he won't do it now. Something changed, something broke. The other Sagemont boys shift their feet on the mangy grass.

"Think about it," Andra says. "You can contact me at my website: w-w-w dot Andra dot com."

Now Josh, he acts embarrassed that she left his team out. He looks away, mumbling, "Maybe . . ." Turns toward his team. "Ready to go, guys?"

I'm impressed, though totally frustrated. Their downsized cap hurls himself into the bus. The Sagemont boys follow, tongue-tied. I still wait for Josh to turn and say something to me, and when Andra moves toward me, I realize it again; it won't happen.

"You wrote me a note," she says.

"Yeah," I say.

"I've been thinking about it."

Huh? What's there to think?

Josh climbs in the bus, but I still can see him. He nods to me through the window: one nod. Then, something shiny rolls to the curb beyond the school fence. That Jag of Andra's, with someone at the wheel. Andra calls me over with her perfect little hand. "That cute boy," she says just for me to hear, "wasn't impressed with your game. If you played a little more defense, you wouldn't have gotten trounced. Maybe that's why he didn't talk to you after the game. . . ."

Huh! What a little snot! Blue eyes, cheerful yet cold, like she's so curious about me—and I'm beginning to think I've got to get her away from me. She gives me the creeps. So I astonish myself, saying, "Look, you came to watch us today, but you made it all into a show about you." Sometimes I really can say it as it is! "I wrote you the note because I thought you might like to join our team. . . ."

Her face tightens.

"Yeah. I'm often asked to join teams, so my dad can buy new balls and outfits."

"Well . . ." I feel caught, a little. That buying new balls bit. "Let's be honest: you don't even try to pretend you're like everyone else."

"Why pretend? It's a lie. We can still help each other."

Meanwhile the Sagemont bus revs and moans away. I glance quickly: the sweaty Sagemonters are at the windows, staring back. By now, everyone's around Andra and me; my team, the fans.

"Look, Andra," I say, "we're not in the same league, not even as schoolmates. You don't need my help. And I don't want yours."

Now she gets what I'm saying, her face narrows, the perfection of her look seems strained. Like her skin, though pretty, is too tight.

"You'll see," she says. "We have more in common than you think."

She spins around, walks off, but says something to Arielle, who had left her bag on the field, dashed to pick it up, and now is running back with it. Arielle replies, like one word. Andra gets in her Jag. Our fans disperse. All the bottled water is gone, so I drink from the fountain and start toward the locker room. I'm bummed out.

"What'd Andra say to you, Arielle?" I ask later, in our school's mangy showers, rubbing lotion on a swollen foot.

"Nothing. 'See you in physics.'"

"Andra taking physics, that's a laugh," I snarl.

"To calculate the rate of acceleration of her Jag to Barney's?"

Grazia steps out of the shower, trying to hide in a towel and dry herself at the same time. She's shy when she's naked in front of us; she developed earlier than the rest of us and it made her self-conscious. She glances at Nikki like, *What's with Lily?*

Nikki says, "She's mad because Andra ruined her action with that Josh guy."

Arielle jumps, eyes glowing. "What action?"

"None," I growl. "Shut up, Nikki."

"Why don't we give Andra a break? It's not easy to be the new girl," says Grazia. Other girls from the team hear this. They hoot. "Yeah, poor Andra. Abersnobbie and Bitch."

"Did he talk to you?" Arielle asks me, as private as can be in the middle of shower steam and shouting.

"No," I say, so curtly, but then I can't stop myself; this is my let-it-all-out day. "Josh *wanted* to talk to me, but who could talk with Andra making such a production? The rich are so needy for attention, it's diseased!"

"Could she be a regular girl, like, when you know her?" asks Grazia, who doesn't give up. "I overheard her talking to Powell." Powell is our lit teacher. "She said all private schools are so phony, she chose to come here to be in a real school."

"What a human being," I scoff. "She told Josh she could recommend him to the Junior National League. Didn't even bother to draw him aside—his whole team could hear it."

Nikki says, "Hey, Lily. All's not lost, relax. You molested Josh all over the field, and he still smiled at you. He liked you, sister, okay? Now chill!" I laugh humorlessly, from pure nervous release.

How could I find out anything about Josh? We just rematched Sagemont. Could we re-rematch? Meanwhile . . . I've got to keep an eye on this Andra creature, I think, and I'm surprised. I don't even know what I mean by that, but my thought has a nasty feel to it.

4

Over the next couple of days, I don't get an opportunity to talk to Andra again, but I'm aware of her, like, all day long. She has such high visibility. And she's making friends quickly. I told you about those two copies of her, the two Barbies. Every day thereafter, her copies spawn other copies. It's like, did we know we had so many blond girls around? Did we care? Now we know, and we care.

So, because guys are like inertia machines—everything takes them a while to figure out—our boy fans aren't all over Andra and her Barbies yet. I give them another week.

So, this morning, Mom chases me out of the house, in panic as usual, even though we live only three blocks from school. No way I could manage to be late. As I walk up to the school, I see Andra arriving in that Jag. A two-door, I notice now.

She's driving. A hulky young guy rides shotgun. I've seen him carry her backpack; I already know his name, Holden. Dressed all in logos. I didn't need to find out his name; the school's becoming like a huge sound track about Andra and all things related to her. So Holden's on the sound track: nineteen, lives at their mansion, something to do with the fact that his parents worked for the Hewlits before. He's hot, by association. If Andra shares him with her copies, maybe they'll spawn more copies together. Andra stops the Jag double-parked. A female cop directing the school traffic wags a finger at her.

Holden hustles around the car's nose, jumps behind the wheel. His hair is built in one cresting wave, and his white K-Swiss don't have a scuff on them. He throws a glance at me, really direct. Like, hey, you and me are the same rank, you down for anything? I beat myself for not giving him the digit. She starts up the footpath. Girls who were cold to her just days ago now hurry to fall in step with her: "Hey, Andra, hey, Andra!"

"Hey," she mouths back, with a pale little smile. She wears Juicies today, matched with Pumas. Again, she looks like a TV ad optically enabled to walk a real crowd, and again, I wonder why she doesn't seem fake and vacuous. She really doesn't. It's an art. I turn into the entrance. She looks at me, straight and focused; then she hurries past and gives me that pale little smile. Before I can even think how to react, she's joined by Tony Meserve, a multiple athlete senior who's six four. I used to have a one-minute crush on him, but he's so rude to everyone, I was honestly afraid he'd embarrass me. Once in the cafeteria, he stared at Nikki's nose hoop and said in front of thirty other kids, "When you blow your nose through that hoop, Nikki, doesn't it snag up with snot?" Nikki died. She hates him forever, calls him the "Aryan Icon." As Andra and Tony slow down, I check her outfit; not Juicies today; they're Crimes and Misdemeanors, the newest hottest brand.

Tony's saying something to Andra. She nods

but looks over her shoulder, catching my eyes fast, like catching a ball.

I walk in after them. What the frick?

Fourth period, English Lit.

I usually like Mr. Powell's rambles on Shakespeare, but today I can't concentrate. When a student aide interrupts class with a note that Padgett wants to see me, I bolt. I love walking the empty hallways during a period. The lockers, all lined up, peaceful, the blue-gray walls, the shellacked linoleum floors that make my sneakers squeak. The emptiness is drab, but it's attractive. It whispers to me that life could be like this—all straight lines, no bad turns. Ms. Padgett's office fills a back corner of the main office. Her door is open; I can see her at her desk, between the American flag and an overgrown rhododendron.

"Hello, Lily," she says. "Come in. Close the door and have a seat."

I close the door, sit in one of the two chairs before her desk. The size of her office doesn't fit her title. Overloaded, messy, but in a way . . . touching. Like, let me grow old here, okay? No pictures on her desk. She never married. Her blue suit hugs her body too tightly. I know what she's going to say: "Lily, we're all impressed with how you and the girls have improved the team spirit and camaraderie here at South Pas." I'll still love hearing it; I deserve my praise.

She says, "Lily, we're all impressed with how you and the girls have improved the team spirit and camaraderie here at South Pas. So I wanted to tell you in person that the school has decided to officially sanction a girls' soccer team."

Oh my God. If we're official, that means uniforms, logo, the whole nine!

"That's amazing, Ms. Padgett. The girls are going to be so excited. Thank you. We've been playing a lot, getting better."

"I know. I read that story in the *Pasadenan,* congratulations."

"Thanks, we've been working hard. It will be a lot easier, now that we're official. More girls will want to join our team now."

"Well," says Ms. Padgett, picking up a pencil and twirling it between her fingers, "that's another reason I wanted to talk to you. The official team is already being formed. I hope you'll agree to join it."

"What?" I choke. "What do you mean, 'already being formed'? By who?"

"Andra Hewlit."

I feel like someone kicked a ball right in my gut.

"Andra?" It's all I can say—my brain's not functioning. When it starts up again, it enables me to mumble, "She's only been a student here, what, three weeks?" I, we, have been here from the beginning of middle school, we *are* this school!

"I know it seems quick, Lily, but it doesn't have to be a bad thing. You and the girls can still be on the team. There's going to be a tryout."

"Tryout?" I scream. Ms. Padgett perks up her brows. I bring my voice down, somehow. With as much sarcasm as I can muster, I say, "Who decides if we make it or not? Andra?"

"And the new coach."

"You're hiring a coach! You said we have budget restrictions! How can you possibly afford to hire a coach?"

She puts the pencil down, slowly. "That's been taken care of. You know, Lily, there's no reason why we couldn't have a club team and an official team, here at South Pas. But the official team will have priority to school equipment and property."

"What property? What do you mean, our field?"

"Yes."

"But we built that field from scratch! Arielle broke her thumb hammering the goalposts! We got it into playing shape, and now we'll have to wait for Andra and her team to be done before we can use it? That's not fair." Ms. Padgett gets up from her chair, because I'm up from mine. She raises her arms as if to say, *What can I do?* and I tell her, "You're the principal here; you're not going to let this happen!"

I shake the air with my indignation; the rhododendron is throbbing in its pot.

"I understand you're upset, but hear me out. We are a small school, Lily, short on supplies." Du-uh! I've had to share toilet paper, give me a break! "So when Mr. Hewlit calls me, says he'll donate a new gym and faculty lounge if Andra gets a team . . . Lily, what would you do in my position? The school district would never allocate funds for all that. . . ."

I cut her off, steaming. "Mr. Hewlit's such a philanthropist, why doesn't he pay to make *my* team official?"

She counters, like, reasonable, "Lily, you're not his daughter—Andra is."

I slump back in my seat. I know. My team's done.

Tears creep up to my eyes while Padgett adds, "It's not a bad thing for you, Lily. You want to play well, you learn from those who already do. Howard—" First name? "—told me that Andra was a nationally ranked player at Millbrook, back in New York. She'll help you girls become really good players, Lily." Pause. I cry silently. "I'll call her in."

Huh?

"She's waiting outside—she asked to be here when I talked to you, but I thought I'd break it to you gently. But she wants you to join, without a tryout for you."

I don't know when I sprung up, when I opened the door.

Yes, in the outer office, Andra sits waiting. Legs crossed, dangling one of those killer Pumas. She's not as ad-like just now; she seems anxious. About what?—she knows she won this one, if she won over the principal. So when I stop before her, hovering so close I give her no room to stand up, she reacts as worried as I've seen her yet, trying to glance around me to see if Padgett's quick to the rescue. Then she looks up into that tear-blurred glare of mine, and for once, she doesn't smile.

I swipe my eyes with my hand. "Why are you

doing this, Andra? You can get yourself your own team anywhere else, even on your back lawn— I'm sure you got one big enough to scrimmage on. If you played Junior National, why don't you join a team in L.A. or San Diego, if you're too good for us?" She tries to reply, but I don't let her. "Me and my friends have our little team, our puny little games. If you start your own team here, all my best players will go over to you—don't you get it? It's not fair."

She recovers her cool. "What's fair, Lily? If I take over the Weregirls, there's a place for you on it. I told you last time, we can help each other. But first, the name of the team. I like Weregirls."

Padgett goes *ahem* behind me, so I step back. Andra gets up, brushing me, almost. Between my battered but clean old sweater and her clothes, there's a few inches' distance, and a whole world. "You can't take over the name," I say. "Me and my friends called ourselves that a bunch of years back."

"It's marketable," she says. "A very good name." As she says it, she looks me in the eyes— am I nuts?—as if she's trying, underneath her words and mine, to tell me, *I* know *what's what. Just can't say it out loud.*

"Oh yes, the name of the team is important,"

says Padgett, calm, back to business. "We insist on the name."

I don't know what happened—Andra's "if I take over" carved itself in my brain. You want to take *me* over, Andra? Then I think. Don't react crazy, Lily, she didn't mean you as a person. But then, eyes wide open, I see across Andra, with her silhouette superimposed on it, like in a movie . . .

I see this:

Mom and I stand by the freshly dug grave into which Dad's coffin is being lowered. The cops fire a salute from rifles held with gloved hands. Mom wears a black suit, and I wear a dress bought for the funeral. I never wore it again after that. Mom throws the first fistful of dirt. Crying behind sunshades. A man I don't know scoops dirt, throws it on the coffin; still in the air, the dirt fans out in a pretty pattern. . . .

The man who threw dirt on the coffin after Mom is old. His hair is dark, braided and knotted at the back of his head. I glimpsed it under his trucker's cap when he leaned over the coffin. Stooped shoulders. Young-looking hair, same color as Dad's. My little friends came to the funeral too, the ones Dad named the Weregirls. Dressed up, pale from crying . . .

I remember the fear. . . . It felt so real, my fear, when Mom went on with the same job that killed Dad. Did my fear ever heal? I don't know. I don't feel it now. Just the anger. Like a thin red filter beyond which I see Dad's funeral, and the girl who challenges me today. Something connects Dad's death with this girl. Yes, she wants the name that my Dad used to call me and my friends. I stand in front of Andra Hewlit. As if liberated. And so angry.

"You want the team name? I'll take *your* name, Andra. Indians have this belief: the names are the souls of people. You take over the Weregirls, I'll take you over. Deal?"

Midway saying it, I think, Why am I talking big? My mom's a patrolwoman saving for me to go to college, I still have to finish school here, my team's history. I couldn't cling even to the name; it's not a brand. Padgett must think right now, Is Lily crazy not to seize this opportunity?

Andra blinks, as if surprised by this, but she also seems excited. She mutters, "Like to like, huh?"

"Huh?" I echo.

She turns to Padgett. "Lily and I will resolve this. Thank you." Padgett is relieved; she nods and steps back behind her desk. Andra says to me, "Lunch, you and me? I could call Holden, to drive us out. . . ." She ponders. "But the caf's okay too; we'll find a quiet spot." She checks the time not by the clicking old clock on the office wall, but by this tiny little gem strapped to her wrist. "In an hour. It'll be good."

She looks animated. Not posing just now. For an instant, she looks like someone I just met, someone I might even like. What do I know about her? Nothing. She might surprise me. I almost hope that she will. "What do you want to talk about, Andra? You're giving up on the team thing?"

"After we talk, you won't want me to." And then she turns and walks out. Just like that, all confidence, although I didn't agree to eat lunch with her—but I didn't disagree either.

I walk out after her. Thinking.

Lunch is in one hour. I got an idea about how to use that hour.

Minutes later, in the editorial room of the *Highlights.*

I'm alone here; everyone else is still in class.

I'm writing a piece for the *Highlights*.

I buzz along, clicking the computer keys, misspelling, correcting. I write till it's all done. Then I reread what I've written:

DO AS I SAY, NOT AS I DO

At the beginning of this school year, Principal Padgett cried lack of funding when four students tried to start a girls' soccer team at South Pas. They could only have a club team. Today, Padgett called in student Lily Willison, founder of the Weregirls, whom you have been cheering for, first skeptically then more and more sincerely, and told Willison that her team is terminated—Andra Hewlit, daughter of the known entrepreneur, was granted permission to form her own official team! If you doubt this, I swear I'm dependable: I'm the Deep Throat of the South Pas athletics tragedy—tragedy because aside from scuttling our team, Padgett is giving up all pretense at role-modeling.

Or maybe . . . she's not!

Maybe she's teaching us a new kind of role-modeling, which is: cajole the rich. Discount the truly meritorious, if they're not wealthy or influential. Why pass on a donation, when all you're asked to do is to discourage your students' idealism while pampering the daughter of a tycoon? Even Tony Soprano would've been a little uneasy with this—in a TV script, I mean. But this is real life. What say you, noble students? You say nothing—you should be abhorred, but all of you want to be on the right team, the official team! Alas, Deep Throat is a thing of the past, a ghost from the consciousness of another time!

PS: How could I forget? Andra also wants the name Weregirls for her team! It's so in character: if you take, take it all! You, the fans of the now gone club team, remember how you cheered them on the field—as themselves. So let them go down in their own name! Please, irregardless, do not address the new team as the Weregirls, do not abet that fraud! From the height of the newly built bleachers, please clamor till hoarse for the new school team, representative and official, the BARBIES!

The Ghost of Deep Throat

I'm amazed. Wow. Anger can be such inspiration!

I reread the piece two more times, just to enjoy it. Great flow. Great consciousness, if I say so myself! Cute turns of phrases too.

Right in time, I access the pages of tomorrow's issue. Early this morning, they were emailed to where our paper is printed—a little print shop still hanging on downtown. But I can still slip this in. I kill a story about "Belated humanitarian efforts reach Darfur"—they're belated anyway, and besides, it's a reprint from the big paper—and I insert "Do As I Say, Not As I Do."

The bell goes. Lunch.

5

In the cafeteria, I get off the loading line with a salad and three slices of white bread on my tray. I'll burn the carbs at practice. That's when I see Andra behind me. She chose a salad and a yogurt.

I start off; she's right behind me. Her Pumas are panther-quiet, like they don't touch the ground. My practice sneakers, ruined and taped, buff the floor with squeaks.

"Hey," she says from behind me. I turn. Her pretty face, turned-up nose, and blue eyes are gleaming from within.

"Hey," I retort.

"So where do we sit down?"

"You choose."

I seem cool, but my voice is raspy. What the hell, Andra Hewlit, now I'll find out what manner of beast you are! But, what about my friends? I never ever had lunch without them. My usual table is now sliding toward me. Seated already, Arielle, Nikki, and Grazia look up, then gawk. Who am I bringing with me? Nikki is opening a soda. She breaks in midaction; the soda bubbles through the half-open tab.

"How about out in the sun?" Andra asks, loud enough for my friends to hear. Then, toward them, "Want to eat outside?" Clearly, there's no risk; they're settled in already, food on their forks, and above all, stunned.

"Where ya at, Lily?" Arielle asks.

"We're eating outside, me and Andra."

Andra walks out with her tray. We're allowed to take trays into the yard, because when some Persian kids hijacked one of our two trees to eat lunch in its shade, we ran a poll in our paper that came back 83 percent, anyone should be allowed to eat outside, it's America here. We mostly don't because there are no tables and chairs outside. The Persians sit on the ground and eat tabbouleh made at home by their moms. I'm still by our table—I haven't even told my friends what Padgett told me about the fate of our team.

Nikki speaks for all three. "Lily, what's this? You're always like, 'Burn the rich,' and now, you're having lunch with Andra?"

"She asked me," I say defensively.

"If I did this, you would've called me a social slut," Arielle says.

Grazia says nothing, but I can tell she's surprised. I don't know how to explain, and there is no time.

"I'll see you all later," I say, and follow Andra out.

I wish I'd worn my better sneakers. These go *swish-swish* with the dirt and rubber melt built up inside them through so many games, doesn't matter how often I wash them. I see Tony Meserve slip out after Andra. Crazy thought: maybe Andra feels guilty for what she set in motion about the team, and will try to soothe me by fixing me up with Tony? Yeah, dream on, Lily! I don't even like Tony anymore. What was that strange excitement in Andra's eyes when she said "like to like"?

I suddenly know what I want, and I want it

badly: I want my team to be the official team. I enjoyed being applauded and cheered, being the school hero. Why should it end so fast? Then I remember Padgett's face, the way she asked me in, so sweetly: close the door, sit down, we are all so proud of you. . . . And I become angry all over again. I walk stumbling, my salad dancing on my tray.

When I make it out to the yard, Andra's sitting on the grass under the "other tree," the one claimed by no ethnic group yet, and Tony leans over her, with a hand clamped on a low branch. "You said you were down to eat lunch with me and the guys. . . ."

"I changed my mind," Andra replies in a thin cool voice.

Tony is really put upon. "Why? What's up?"

"I'm having lunch with Lily. She and I have interests in common."

I approach with my tray. Tony looks at me while Andra inspects her yogurt.

"How's kickball, Lil?"

He never even says hello to me, and now I'm Lil?

"Fine. Want to eat with us?"

"I thought we were talking, Lily," Andra says

promptly. I could giggle. Tony looks like he was doused with water! He turns and huffs off.

From the mood I was in while writing that incendiary piece for the paper, I begin to slide back to normal. Andra wants something from me, definitely—what does she want?

Again, that other part of me whispers, Patience. You'll find out.

"So," I say as I break a piece of bread, put it in my mouth, "what are our common interests?"

"Soccer, among other things." Andra shifts her body on the grass, closer to me, puts her hand on my arm. "Don't cast a spell on me before you hear me out. I'm not supernatural, nor magical, not at all." She says it like she would say "I'm not musical," or "not practical." "Come on, Lily, don't play dumb. I know you have magical powers."

I look at her like, *Who's the loon here, you or me?*

"Fine," she says. "I figured you'd be like that. That's why I took matters into my own hands. I knew this one thing that's so important for you: the team. You can have your team; there's room for both of us, Lily. You can be my cocaptain, or I yours," she adds hastily, "if you teach me about your secret powers."

Is she joking?

But her voice is totally serious, not even mocking. "Where'd you get that name, Weregirls?"

I explain, "It's a nickname. My dad gave it to me and my friends when we were little girls."

She smiles. She is excited; her hand on my arm grips more tightly. "Precisely, your father. I know a little something about him."

For a split second, that memory I had in Padgett's office, me at Dad's burial, fills my mind again. Andra is talking. "You shouldn't take me for a dodo; I've traveled round the world and back. I still love New York the best. It's so spooky. You can't get spooked in Pasadena anywhere, not even alone at night in the Metrorail tunnel." I wonder, has she been inside that tunnel? I free my arm.

"I was practically in New York when they smashed the towers. We have a house in Long Island, right across the bay. I stared at that hellish smoke over the bay; for a month I didn't even go shopping. So I *know fear.* You do too," she adds, as if to assure me that I'm not inferior. "Your dad was shot dead, how lamentable." She's got good vocab too, that other voice comments inside me.

"Two weeks ago, the chief of police and his wife came to dinner at our house."

I shrug. "And?"

She puts her tray on the grass. I do too.

She continues, with a slight hardening in her voice, "I want you to know this: New York turned against my father after he made everyone there a ton of money. Anyway, we're back here, and my mom wants to be active in the community. She might run for the board of education, so it helps to have the city notables over for dinner. The night the police chief and his wife came over, I was out. I got back after they'd finished eating, and went into the kitchen to fix myself something. You can hear everything from the kitchen. The chief was saying, 'Yeah, the worst is when we face things we have no training for, like five years ago, when those so-called conjurers took over an abandoned block downtown. We had an officer infiltrate them.' And then the chief's wife said, 'Matt Willison didn't give you all the information about that gang.' The chief said, 'Of course he didn't give me the information; he was protecting them. But I'm still sorry he died, and left a wife and a kid.' Then my mom asked, 'What are conjurers?'

The chief said, 'I don't know exactly . . . people with magical powers, spells, whatever. . . .' "

I say nothing. I get so quiet, I hear voices arguing inside the cafeteria.

"Hey." Andra gently pats my arm. "Was your father working undercover?"

I whisper, "Yes . . ."

And again, I see.

I stand by the fresh trench into which Dad's coffin is being lowered. The cops fire a salute. The shots crack hard. That older man throws dirt on the coffin, the dirt hits the coffin's lid, and . . . fear strikes my heart. From being only a word, death becomes *death*. It took my dad. It could take me. Then . . .

Everyone comes to our house. Men and women I don't know, almost all police, drink shots of whiskey in memory of Dad, chew food that was brought in, hug Mom and me. Strangers' hugs, unwanted. The man who threw dirt on the coffin, he's here too. . . . I feel his eyes on me. . . . I sneak a glance, to memorize his carved face. He has such pain in his eyes, it adds to my pain. . . . Mom, heal my pain. Mom, vanquish my fear. . . .

Can I say any of this? Can I say it to Andra

Hewlit, today, now? I never even said it to myself. Mom, you still putting on that bulletproof vest? Today, like back then? You say you don't know how to do anything else, that it's for your daughter. It might heal your daughter. Well, I'm healed. What now?

I turn to Andra; she's still talking. "The chief's wife was drunk. She started to rag like, 'Matt Willison could've sunk the department, and you with it.'"

I feel a cramp in my gut. I hear a whizzing sound in my ears.

"The chief said, 'Willison was a good detective. It's terrible that things ended as they did.' Then his wife said, 'Willison was one of them.' And the chief said, 'Shut up, Wendy. What are you trying to make me say?'"

I grab Andra's arm. "Who else was there, and heard this?"

Andra knits her brows. "My brother was out. Holden was in the den, watching TV. . . ."

"The guy who drives you to school? Who is he?"

"No one." It can hit hard, that thin voice of hers! "Our valet—not like in parking cars." Andra smiles, as if glad to lighten the conversation. "I don't know what he heard; I don't really speak to him. Our cook was running back and forth, but he never pays any attention except for how people like his food. I'm sure my parents didn't pay attention; this was dinner chat. When people come to our house, they try to impress my parents. When they can't talk about how much money they have, they show off any other way they can."

"Like, the chief showed off about my dad being killed?"

She nods. "Killed while protecting a gang, but not some dope-dealing bunch—they had magical powers. After the chief snapped at his wife, she got so flustered, she said, 'I'm not one of your subordinates,' and he apologized, and my mom called me to help serve the liqueurs. Where are you going, Lily?"

I get up and pick up my tray. Untouched, except for one bite of bread.

I face her with the tray in my hands. "My dad was a respected officer. He worked undercover— you have to be trusted for that. Maybe those people weren't conjurers, but just unusual, or misunderstood. Anyway, is this why you're so interested in me? You heard someone's drunk garbage, so you drag me out here to imply what, that my dad protected criminals? He would've never done that."

"No, no." She sounds truthful, somehow. "That's not it at all. . . . Lily . . ."

She tries to touch my arm again, but I pull out of her reach. She speaks fast. "I totally don't care, even if they had records. In New York, when we had people over, some were out on bail for insider trading. So what. We all do what we have to do. . . ."

Through a walkway between two buildings, this yard connects with the front lawn and the street. I don't want my friends to see me walk back into the caf choking with anger. So I'll follow the walkway out.

I start walking. She bolts, hurries after me.

"Lily? I don't care about what the chief said . . . and I won't repeat it either. But it's like a light went on in my head when I remembered the story in the *Pasadenan,* and the name of your team." She did an encircling move, blocking off the walkway. She lowers her voice. "Weregirls."

"Yeah, that's our team's name. So?"

A sly expression lights up her face. "I have some books on magic, one quite old—it mentions the weregirls. I never found them mentioned anywhere else." As I walk faster, she almost runs after me. "If you let me in on the magic, Lily, you could be my friend with benefits. Do you know what that means? Clothes, guys, fun, the team—whatever you're into, I'll give it to you."

I stare at her, reconnecting the dots. "So after you thought out all that, you had your father ask Padgett to give you an official team?"

She's kind of pleased with herself. "I knew I wouldn't get your attention otherwise."

I could knock her to the ground. She's no match for me.

"I'm not supernatural," she insists. "I recognize that—but I'm fast and determined, I can handle people, we could be the greatest pair together—"

I cut her off. "It's all in your head."

"But the chief said—"

"Shut up!" I shout.

Then I charge through to the front lawn, where I change direction like when dribbling a ball. Somehow, I lost my food tray. I can't turn back to look for it; Andra's hot behind me. "Lily? Are you turning me *down*? If you must know, kids from all over the world want to be my friends. Any time I come back from vacation, I find dozens of hits on my website. More girls than boys, even." Maybe a shadow darkens my face, for she hurries to add, "I'm not like, into chicks, if that's what worries you. I'm really interested in—"

"Go to hell!"

I slip inside.

But I spy her through one of the entrance door's glass panes.

She turns and heads back to the inner yard, crossing the lawn. Halfway, she stops and stomps the grass with her foot, in a show of anger she doesn't know I'm watching.

I stand in the hallway, thinking.

I start to walk again. Berating myself for having sat with her as long as I did. Without even showing how angry I was. I should've cracked open that salad dressing and slung it at Andra's coiffed hair.

Then something grabs at my heart—this was about my dad. I hadn't thought about him in a while. Too filled with soccer, girlfriends, girl desires. *Officer Willison was into . . . things cops shouldn't be into. . . .* I get so angry, I kick at a locker's graffitied face.

"Psssttt! Lily!"

I jump. Nikki's in front of me.

Ahead, down the hall, the door to a class—Mr.

Guttierez's Spanish class—is wide open. My class-mates are at their desks, writing. Mr. Guttierez leaves the doors open during tests.

Nikki whispers, "I turned in the test blank, so I could get out and look for you. Jesus, Lily! We saw you from the caf's window, storming off with Andra. You looked like you could eat her liver. What did she do to you?"

I grab control. "Nothing." I touch my hair. It's exploding. I pat it down. My forehead is wet.

I'm ready to spew it all out. But I stop myself, picturing Nikki's gawking face when I mention the chief. . . . No, I can't share this, even with my best friend.

At Dad's funeral, that same chief said in a pious voice, looking up from a typed page, "Matt Willison, remember us, for we'll never forget you—you're unforgettable and irreplaceable." Yet, five years later, at a rich people's dinner . . . *Matt Willison could've sunk the whole department.* . . .

Nikki keeps on it. "What did she say to you?"

I grit my teeth. "Nikki, I don't want to tell you now!"

But Nikki's like, "You've got to. Come on."

"Later!" I yell, turn, and storm out.

6

I stagger into downtown South Pas. Somehow,
like a flicker of rationality inside madness, I
remember: it's Nikki's birthday tomorrow. I
wanted to come here to buy her something.

These shopping alleys. They never change. Doug-
las, and Bonham, and Smith Alley, named for capi-
talists who got rich selling survival items in the
early West. Saddles, guns, harnesses for coaches.
Justice was easy. They didn't like you, they hanged
you high. Those saddle-and-gun stores are now the
Armani Exchange, Victoria's Secret, Ikono, X-eez,
stores that Andra could afford—I hoof it to Urban
Outfitters to buy spaghetti-string panties, which I
insist on wearing but no one sees them. At Urban

Outfitters, they're three for twelve dollars. I gotta get something cool for Nikki, but not too girly—she'd flip. She hasn't worn a skirt since grade school.

All the alleys have bars and restaurants. Ideal for when kids come out of a movie, in narrow alleys where a police cruiser can't enter, trees and benches, ideal for hooking up. It used to be that a guy picked up a girl at her place. He'd walk in, meet the parents, and they'd make him take the you-don't-touch-my-baby oath while he thought of nothing else but touching her. Ditto the girl, who'd be fixing herself up upstairs. Then she'd come down, he'd take her out, and spend dollars!

That was then. Now, it's like, boys and girls go to a movie, to Coffee Bean, bowling, whatever. A girl and a guy feel the attraction, and slip away together. He can be all hands, she can be all hands too—I guess for a girl it can be fascinating, to see a guy turn into a clumsy animal *because of you.* And it's all okay. A certain limit is respected, sort of—just think what happened in a recent White House, all kids know about that—and that's hooking up. No real feelings involved. And they don't talk about it after it's over. If they like it, they're "friends with benefits," meaning they can do it again. If they didn't like it, no one finds out but the guy's best friends of course, and the girl's best friends, and it's still okay. Girls refer to hooking up as "CTAW"—cleaner than all the way. Who cares that the guy gets (almost) all he wants, without shelling out a single dollar. Anatomically, it's like it didn't happen. What an improvement. Who needs feelings?

I speak with some (theoretical) authority. I researched hooking up. I wrote an editorial for the *Highlights* titled "Death before Hooking-Up," which Harris approved for publication if I changed the title to "Say No to Promiscuous Dating." So lame. But Harris was so freaked by the title, he never got to censor the story, and I had some racy quotes. "Hooking up is fun, nothing beats it in variety," said junior Arielle Knelling— she really did say it, though she didn't even know what she was talking about, except for one time. So I quoted her. "But real feelings may get involved, and then people get bruised," cautioned Grazia Barbieri. *I* wrote Grazia's quote, to balance out Arielle, but it's okay—Grazia would say something like that. But the best quote was from Tony Meserve. Hold yourselves. "High school's the training ground for later relationships," opined senior Meserve, "but hooking up is like boot camp—it can be brutal, and not on the girls only." Wow, Tony, you're so deep!

Of course, *I* wrote his quote, every word. And read it to him before publication. Expecting that he'd want to have lunch with me in the caf, grateful to me for his improved image as a thinking being, right? "I'm not down for lunch, but print what you want, Lily," he said. So I gave him the number to my cell—in case he changed his mind about being quoted, I told him. He digited my number into his BlackBerry. "Yo, later." He didn't call, didn't even nod hello the day my editorial was out.

But the editorial was a hit—the students tore the paper to read it. "You got legs *and* brains, Lily," a senior told me. "Except for the lame ending, 'Let's return to old-fashioned love'—Harris made you put that in, right?" No, that was still me! I'll go through life rolling my eyes. When I'm me, they don't get it; when I'm not me, they get it, for the wrong reasons.

One more thing I wrote as the conclusion of the piece: if sexual attraction is based on looks, that's *profiling*. We're after, like, thousands of years of sexual profiling. But if we all closed our eyes, and let ourselves be led by smell, touch, taste, hearing, speed (is speed one of the six senses?—like, how fast the guy moves on you?), wouldn't we choose the least expected partners?

I'm having this fantasy. The world is pairing up with eyes closed, and I kiss a guy, peep my eyes open, see *everyone* paired with their deadliest opposites (Nikki is with the Aryan Icon, Tony!), and I'm with . . . Josh from Sagemont! I swear I'm surprised!

In my left pocket, my cell throbs against a bruise from last practice. I whip it out. Nikki's number's on the screen. "Hello?"

"Lily? Where are you?"

I yelled at Nikki before blowing out of school. Now I whine humbly, "Passing Johnny Rocket's, in the alley. . . . Hey, you all cut Spanish?"

"School's over, dummy, d'you know what time it is? Hey, Lily, Andra's standing right by me. . . ."

"What? What's Andra doing there?"

"Andra wants to speak to you."

An anxiety like a jabbing headache hits me. Why is that idiot there? What does she want? Panic. Is she telling my friends what the chief of police said about my dad? Leaning on Johnny Rocket's, I peer in a window. Three cooks rolling meat patties with their hands, no plastic gloves, *nada.*

Through clenched teeth: "What does she want, Nikki?"

"She said it's personal. What secrets you got with her all of a sudden?"

"No secrets. Nikki, I can't tell you more just now."

Nikki, very cutting: "Maybe I'll ask Andra."

The slimy octopus of fear moves inside me. I want to grab the corner of Johnny Rocket's and retch. Why so much fear? Andra said crazy stuff; no one would believe it. . . . And yet I stammer, "Don't ask her, Nikki. It's not important. . . . Tell her you couldn't find me. . . ."

"Uh-huh," says Nikki. "Like the Chinese say, 'Save your best manners for your family; they're your lifelong friends.' "

"Nikki? Hold on." I was supposed to talk to my mom around this time. Just then, *oom-oom,* another call. Parents are punctual! I press the button, shape up my voice. "Mom?"

"Lampert," a male voice says. Mom's boyfriend, patrolman Tim Lampert. "Lily? Why aren't you answering your phone? Your mom was looking for you." He's talking from the police car; I can tell by the sound.

I grunt, "Uh-huh, I was just going to call her. Is she with you?"

"No. She worked late, so she just went home. Lily, is anything wrong?" He always tries to go parental on me; it drives me crazy.

"No, Tim. I was just going to call Mom."

"It's okay, Lily, I just called her myself, told her I saw you on the field at practice. Why worry her?"

"Uh-huh."

"My pleasure." Mellifluous, like, *You want a new dad?* Ugh, stop it, you got Mom in the sack already, so stop this sucking up to the daughter, it's disgusting and unnecessary! "So long, Tim." I hang up quick.

I click back to Nikki's number. Busy. I try Arielle, get her optimistic message: "Hi, I'm dying to talk to you, but I'm busy just now—leave your name and number." At sixteen, Arielle and Grazia are still very good-natured, but Nikki and I are turning into these jagged nails. I hang up, try Grazia: "Hi, you reached—" Damn. I try Nikki again.

"Hey," says Nikki. "Where was I?"

"Uh . . . Doling out wisdom about Chinese family customs?"

"Well you've been so rude to me today."

"I'm allowed to be rude; you're not my sister."

Oops! Now I could slap myself. When Nikki and I became friends I had both parents. She'd lost hers in a boating accident—she already lived with that uncle and aunt. After my dad died, Nikki was so sweet to me, accompanying me protectively to school, telling off the kids who asked insensitive questions, really like a sister. So I've just been horrid, and she deals it back. "You know what, Lily? Have your meltdown by yourself, I'm nexting you!" Bam, the line goes dead. But then Grazia calls. "Lily, what's going on? You're not yourself."

"I'm sorry. Andra made me feel real bad, but I didn't want to burden you all. . . ."

Grazia laughs. "When the hell did you not burden us?"

It's hard to be mad at Grazia, who's always sweet and friendly. She's round and plump like a nymph in an old painting, but is not at all hung up about it. We went to the Norton Simon Museum on a field trip once, and saw Grazia in a million versions, as Venus sleeping, and Venus awake teasing Cupid, as Europa Raped by the Bull, and Leda and the Swan (it seems that Renaissance people were into animal sex). By present standards, all the nudes were overweight. So I sidled up to Tony Meserve, who yawned with some other seniors. "You think these models look like my friend Grazia?" (Who *is* Italian—that curvaceousness must be from generations of pasta!) He went, "Which one is she?" I pointed her out to him—Grazia had her clothes on of course, but her round cheeks, clear skin, and curly brunette hair were gorgeous, if you took a second to appreciate them. He looked back at me. "Yeah, you're thinner than her, Lily." Like that's what I wanted him to notice!

I shake myself to the present. "Put Andra on, I'll speak with her."

"Andra just left."

And I was so ready to listen to Andra apologizing to me! But I made her wait too long! The super jerk, she got in her Jag and drove off!

I snap, "How could you let her walk away like that? Get everyone on!" Which means, they'll all huddle around Arielle's cell, because Arielle's cell's got a speaker—her unprosperous journalist dad works part-time in this electronics store where we all got new cells at incredibly low prices. So now that all four of us are on together, I unload: "Andra's dad is bribing Padgett to give Andra her own team." I stop to allow them to growl: *Wha-at?! Wow!!*

"Yeah, and she made me feel so *poor,* my dad took bullets for her kind, the ones who always benefit, the rich, and Andra is interested in, guess what? The supernatural. She thinks we have magical powers, that even our team name has magical powers—she found it mentioned in a book. So she wants our team name too! She totally bought off Padgett. But I wrote this anonymous piece about Andra and Padgett, and slipped it into the next *Highlights,* let everyone know!" This gets them quiet; then Nikki says, "Right on," but Arielle says, "Oh my God," and Grazia says, "They'll figure it was you and they'll throw you out of school, Lily. Call the office, call Harris, tell him it was a joke!"

"Hey, what the hell . . ." I wipe my forehead. I'm sweating like at practice. But I still cling on. "Let it happen, Grazia. If they can't take a joke . . ."

But Grazia says what I'm thinking. "You can't do this to your mom, Lily."

I'm stammering, "Andra deserves it, and Padgett; they both do. . . . You know what she dared to imply about my dad?"

But Grazia, who's so less flamboyant and soft-spoken usually, now she's untamable. "Lily! Now!"

I click off with the girls. I call the school office. But Harris just left, and they won't give out his cell or home number. I call the girls back. Now I'm scared.

"Call the print shop," Grazia says, cool under fire.

Now I'm panicking. I picture the press wheels rolling. I gotta stop the press wheels from rolling, or Mom's going to ground me forever.

I call information, get the print shop's number, call the print shop. I speak to the manager. I describe the crisis. That earlier story, about the humanitarian efforts finally reaching Darfur, must be reinserted. Too topical to be left out. The manager sounds like an older guy, not impressed with my urgency. They didn't start printing yet. They'll substitute the earlier story, no prob. He'll supervise the process himself. I hang up.

I call the girls back; they get on the speaker. "Thanks," I say. "I would've been dead."

"No," Grazia says. "You would've been Andra's best friend, all of a sudden. 'Cause it sounds like Andra's not just taking over the team, she's taking over the school."

"The rich bought out the revolution," mumbles Nikki, who collects vintage Che and Mao buttons. "Instead of butting heads with Andra, let's get her to buy us cleats."

Arielle betrays me too. "Yeah, I'm tired of playing in sneakers. Can you mend it with her, Lily?"

"Why not?" says Arielle. "Andra was trying to talk to Lily just one second ago. What did you tell her, Lily, that we place spells before practice? Before every penalty shot, I spell the ball to score—and then, *voom*?"

"Girls," I plead. "Andra believes it. This is her reality plane."

"In that case, she could be like a project for us," Nikki says. "Come on, Lily, don't be a softie." *Whaaa . . . ?* Nikki takes it to the goal line: "She gets team, you get co-captain, we all get personalized Puma cleats."

No, it can't be. Not after what she said about Dad. But, she didn't . . . The police chief's wife said it, and she told me she didn't even care. Look at this: I'm ready to give her a break myself. Like to like. Suddenly, I remember that Andra said that: like to like. . . . But what was the meaning? What was the context?

Grazia says, "Hey, Lily, I see my dad's truck. You want us to pick you up?"

Uh . . . Be picked up in a pizza truck, while Andra drove off in a Jag? But Mom picks me up in her cruiser, which is another utilitarian vehicle, and I never felt self-conscious about that before. Damn Andra, she's infecting my mind! Even if it's not my style, I'm no softie, so I gush, "Hell yes, pick me up. I'm rich. I got you girls as friends! Nikki? Are you there? I was a jerk to you today. I'm sorry."

"Me too," she says. "The matter's closed."

"Then we all meet at the mall tonight?" asks Arielle.

"Sure," I say.

I look out to the street. Seconds later, I see the pizza truck.

Later, at home.

Mom's asleep. I have the kitchen and den to myself.

I keep thinking about it. Say I make up with Andra, maybe we even start socializing with her, will she tell the girls about the po chief? Not if I ask her not to. I picture her pale smile: *Sure, Lily.*

This dies with me. But just between us, what kind of magic was your dad into? Black magic, I hope? That's the hottest!

My mind moans, and I'm reinvaded by that squiddy, disgusting fear. Like to like . . . There's something that comes back to me, when I think about those words, I've heard them before, maybe?

Come on, I tell myself. Come on. Who knows what that idiot meant? I for one don't know a lot about the supernatural, or about magic, nothing really, so why should I feel that it's a negative? My dad didn't think that it was, of that I'm certain. Classic literature is full of witches, good and bad. Shakespeare, witches. Peter Pan, elves and fairies. I don't want to flick on the TV just now, because I know what'll lunge out of it, right at me: ghosts, vampires, aliens. My thoughts wander off, and I'm suddenly sad and lonely. What's the matter with me?

It's simple. I miss my dad. So much.

7

Two days later—Saturday

Nikki's birthday is today, so basically everything else goes on hold. She's turning sixteen, the youngest of us. Yesterday, she categorically forbade us to give her a sweet sixteen party. "That mainstream stuff is so totally limp, it's like programming for future Stepford wives," she said.

"All right," I said, "we still have practice tomorrow." We practice every Saturday.

So Nikki comes to practice this morning, and everyone's there. The team, other friends, the team's moms. Even my mom comes, in sweats, Sunday style, and everyone's relaxed and casual. I order the girls to form teams as if for practice.

Nikki stations herself on the offense line, I blow my whistle—one team mom paces over, arms filled with this chocolate cake in the shape of a soccer field and team. (I got it at Personalized Cakes; it cost a murderous $36.) Among the tiny chocolate players, there's Nikki, identifiable through a Lilliputian hoop of wire that Arielle tweezed and fitted with infinite care in Nikki's chocolate nose. Nikki's right foot brushes a ball made of a brown raisin. Along one touchline, I wrote with white topping, *Happy Sweet Sixteen Nikki!*, and along the other touchline *The Toughest Sweetest Offense in the World!*

Nikki twists her face—I think she'll spit on the cake. But instead . . . she starts to cry.

"Girls," she moans, "this is . . . this is . . ."

We don't let her totally embarrass herself, but pile up on her, knock her down on the grass, and when she's down there, still crying, we pour our little bags of gifts on her. Girly girl stuff: CDs, makeup and makeup accessories, with the receipts in the bags. We're taking a chance with the makeup, just like we did with the cake and the whole thing. We also give her a framed photograph of the team with her in the middle next to me, a teddy bear in a soccer shirt and shorts, and a LIVE STRONG bracelet, of brass, not rubber, which makes her cry even more.

In short, the load. Some of the moms get weepy too, so Nikki blows her nose and says, "Come on, let's practice! And then we eat the cake!"

"It's your day, Nikki," I say. And then, we all play fantastic!

Then we eat the cake on the field, every scrap.

Mom finds a moment to whisper to me, "You're so lucky, Lily. You have the greatest friends. Don't ever betray them."

"Gee, Mom, you know I won't. Why would you say something like that?"

"I meant nothing by it, sweetie." She pats my arm.

I warned her that Tim couldn't come, this was an all-girls affair, so she came alone. Good. When Tim's not around, Mom's almost the mom I knew. But when he's present, she fusses, smiles too much, and primps herself like she never did for Dad. In Dad's time, she never used products on herself except for shampoo and soap. She's still a knock-out when she steps out of her cruiser, in her 911 blue: the blade of her cap sectioning her face above her brown eyes, her nose, lips, chin so delicately chiseled, wafting out cool, coiled-up power. Ready to spring. Speaks softly: Sir, would you show me your driver's licence, *please*? Step out of the car, *please*? Now turn and face the wall, *please*? Your hands behind your back, sir, yes, *like that, please*? And click, the cuffs. Iced fire. Yeah, Mom!

Even now, wearing over-laundered old sweats, she's so taut and trim and terrific, no other mom can hold a candle to her. But when Tim's around, she rushes to make him coffee (makes me mad, thinking of the coffee she made for Dad, always laced with hostility), and when Tim reaches to hug her, she nestles into him, obeisant, willing! Weak! While he, like an uncrowned king, looks at our backyard with confident eyes. "Someone should finish up this pool, don't you think, Marcia?"

I always hurry to respond. "I'm finishing it, Tim. It's my project."

"You never have the time," Tim says.

"Look, I got all the tiles on the bottom. All I have to do is finish the sides and lay wood planks around the top."

"You don't know how to work wood," Tim says.

"I do. I built the gates on our field."

Stopping Tim from taking over Dad's work, it's like Dad's still around, a little. I know why I haven't finished the pool, although I could get the girls together, and in a week we'd be done. I don't want Mom and Tim together in Dad's pool.

Aaugh, enough about Tim! To finish celebrating Nikki's birthday, the four of us are going out Sunday night. Grazia's taking us, on her allowance from the pizzeria cash register.

So. It's Sunday night, at a place called Tapas, and the night turns unexpectedly crazy. We're not wearing dresses because Nikki doesn't own a dress. Just our best knockoff jeans. Nikki smeared herself with makeup and looks weird. A Russian waitress eager for a tip whispers to us, "You want a Coke with vodka, in Coke glass? Color same, no one can tell. What, you 'fraidy cats? You American power girls! In Russia, girls no power. I bring?"

"No thanks," I say. "We're not old enough. We don't want to get you in trouble."

She laughs a big cracked laugh. "My trouble is my trouble. I bring."

In no time, she brings a tall brimming drink on a tray: Coke with vodka. In the adumbrated lighting of Tapas, it looks just like a Coke. We glance at each other. This is a first. "Dribble that ball," Nikki says, and slurps a little, and then pushes the glass around the table.

"Happy sixteen, Nikki." Arielle slurps too, and sneezes.

"Don't sneeze in the drink," says Grazia, then she takes a sip too, pushes the drink to me. I sip. It burns my throat. "I don't get why guys are into drinking."

"I don't get why guys are into anything," Nikki outbids me.

We laugh and feel that was very funny. Then we feel sad.

The Russian waitress is watching. Smiling. "Now you real power women. More?"

"Maybe later," I say.

She laughs and leaves. Nikki stares after her.

"Power women," Nikki grumbles. "In America, the power of women is gone—the women themselves are giving it up. They want kids and suburban life and one-salary families; they want the hubbies to take care of them." She looks around at the other tables. Tapas is full—dating couples, couples with infants sedated in strollers. "Is this what we're headed for?"

"It's life, Nikki."

"Not for us," says Nikki fiercely. "We've got to do something to put us ahead of this pitiful crowd." She's getting loud. "To defeat our fears, to give us direction. . . . You're the cap of the team, Lily, you come up with it."

"I don't know what you're talking about."

"I'm talking about how we could get a little power."

"Power to do what?" The glass of vodka/Coke sits in front of me, empty.

"To handle things. From getting grades, to dumping guys."

"I want to fall in love," I say. "With an average kid, with a big shirt that belonged to his older brother, who says, let's watch some old Kurosawa movie on tape. Who *talks to me,* not just, yo, whatup, uh-huh, hunh?"

I feel emotional. I don't know why.

"Just an okay guy who's a little romantic," I say. "That's all I want, and if it knocks me down like the flu, so be it."

"But we gotta get some insurance against the heartache," says Nikki. "The only insurance is power." I utterly understand. On some profound level, Nikki makes perfect sense. "So if Mr. Dream Guy walks in just now and sees you, you make him do what *you* want him to do."

"You direct his thought paths." Arielle laughs, and sneezes again.

"Yeah," yells Nikki. "Lily, find us that power!"

"Me?" I gurgle.

"Your dad knew magical stuff! You told us!"

"All right! Quiet down, team! All right!"

The wing of fear touches me. Its touch is soft. There's something almost pleasant in being brushed by it. Like being taken over . . .

"Fake it, Lily," Arielle says, and we all laugh. And then Grazia, who sits facing toward Tapas's counter, says, "Is that your guy, Lily?"

My guy? But I spin around—we all do, like zebras at a watering hole.

Tapas's counter has a spot marked "pick up." Josh from Sagemont stands there, speaking to a waiter. He looks taller than he had on the field, and his hair is longer than I remember it—it brushes his cheeks. As he combs it back with his fingers, light fills his eyes. Now I can really look at him: strong nose, with a high bridge, lips full. The waiter moves his hands uneasily. Grazia guesses: "They messed up his order."

"What's he doing in town? Lily, go bring him to our table," says Nikki.

I squirm. "I only saw him once before. . . ."

"I don't care, it's my birthday. Go on, live ball, on the offense!"

"Shut up!" I falter. He's seen us.

He leaves the counter, weaves his way among the tables toward us. I glance at my friends. Their radars register: approaching male. Nikki swallows: radar, lock on. Grazia sits up, letting her boobs point out. Usually self-conscious about their size, she sits with her shoulders turned in. Now she's bulging out: radar, lock on. Arielle flutters her hair and laughs loud for absolutely positively no reason: radar, lock on. Yes, he's very handsome. I suck in my stomach: radar, lock on.

"Hey," he says, "I'm Josh, remember me?" A collective giggle from all four of us. "How's the team doing?"

"What's left of it." Arielle dives in so brusquely, I gawk. Speaking fast, glowing—the vodka? "That rich tart you saw on our field, the school's giving her an official team." She checks me with a quick glance. "Lily's so upset." I crumple the edge of the tablecloth. What the hell is Arielle doing? I don't need her to speak for me! "That girl even wants to take over our team name. . . . She's crazy." Arielle stops. Josh looks at her, then back at me.

Nikki asks him, "You want a Coke with vodka in it?"

"Uh . . . I'm just picking up some takeout."

"It's my birthday," Nikki announces. "So sit a minute, pull a chair."

Wow! This is, like, betrayal en masse for totally opportunistic personal hormonal goals! But I pinch my lips, and wait through Josh asking permission for an empty chair from a table of gay execs with hair glued up in fish scales. He brings the chair, sits, and the Russian waitress materializes.

"I'll have a ginger ale," he says, and the waitress looks at me like, *With the real stuff in it?* I could just nod yes. How would Josh react? I shake my head. She marches off scornfully. I'm such a chicken. No wonder I haven't hooked up.

I finally talk. "What are you doing in Pasadena?"

"Visiting with my dad. He and my mom split up, now he works as a contractor, mostly away from home. This week he's in a trailer down here. There's some slum he's knocking down. He told me if I want to skip a year of school, he'll hire me. I don't know, it's money."

"You having dinner with your dad?"

"Yeah." The ginger ale comes; he takes a sip.

"You look so buff, do you lift weights?" Arielle asks, with the most obvious goo-goo eyes on the planet. He doesn't ignore her, but . . . I'm positive, his real attention is on *me*. He looks at me while answering Arielle. "Yeah. Mostly I'm eating better. I used to smoke in the desert with other guys. I stopped that."

He combs his fingers in his hair; his arm swells like a block and pulley. Everything about him seems larger. I get that nervous girl feeling: a strong male is beautiful, but he could cripple you—but was any girl ever slowed down by that thought? I'm not either. Josh's shirtsleeves are rolled up. Arms like pipes. On his right forearm, I glimpse a tattoo: in tiny black silhouette, wolflike creatures harass a round object. A soccer ball. Small tattoo, but artfully detailed. The creatures' dotlike eyes seem to be twinkling, and their mouths grin joyously. Their bodies are gray-blue, but the soccer ball is yellow, resembling a tiny moon.

Branded on Josh's arm, the weregirls are playing soccer.

I vaguely feel like I've seen this before. But I don't remember where.

Josh notices that I'm looking at his tattoo. "I just got this," he says. He leans his arm on the table.

Instantly, my girlfriends are all over it. Arielle squints her eyes as if feeling his pain. "This must've hurt." She rubs a finger on his skin.

"Not that much," Josh says.

Grazia leans over the table. "Where'd you get it?"

"San Diego." He smiles. "Just after our rematch, we played San Diego. After the game, our bus broke down, so I walked into a tat place just to kill time. This tat guy showed me a book of patterns, and I thought this one was unusual, asked what it was. He said these are the weregirls playing ball. I remembered your team name." He meets my eyes. All of a sudden, my heart starts to pound fast. I glance back for the waitress—maybe I'll have another Coke!

"Your last name's Willison, right? The tat guy said he used to be a cop, he was partners with a Matt Willison—your dad, right?" I nod. When you want those waitresses, they're never there.

"He also showed me a clipping from a newspaper. . . ."

Nikki catches on. "The *Daily Pasadenan*?"

"Yeah." He's still looking only at me. "It said in that story, your dad taught you how to play."

"Lily's dad was a cool guy," says Arielle. She bends again to look at Josh's arm. It has fine brown hairs. Those wolfish creatures prance on his skin, sweet puppyish beings, nudging the moon.

Josh is still facing toward me only. "Your dad got shot in the line of duty?"

I nod. I still get that rough feeling, because kids always ask that with a kind of excitement. I breathe, "That tat guy, did you ask him his name?"

"No, I didn't think about it."

"Don't worry about it." I point to his arm. "Did he draw this?"

"He had it in a book of patterns, with a whole section on soccer. He even had Pelé scoring for the Santos team."

Now we whoop. Pclé! Edson Arantes do Nascimento! The Black Pearl, he won the World Cup for Brazil, scoring a thousand goals in 999 first-class matches! Then he was hired for millions by a New York–based team, Cosmos, and led them to victory too!

"You chose this over Pelé?"

"Yeah. The guy started talking about your dad, and I couldn't believe the coincidence—we had just played you. I like coincidence. So I said, yeah, carve me with this one."

The waitress reappears, but now I forgot what I wanted from her. "Did he mention how my dad died?"

"No." He shifts in his seat.

Arielle says quickly, "We could put this tat on our shirts, as our team insignia. . . . If we still have a team. . . ." She throws her hair around again. "The moon's a magical soccer ball . . . but the moon's also erotic, right?" Josh shrugs. Now he looks at Grazia. "Hey, goalie," he says.

Grazia smiles. Then she stares at me like, *Get off your butt, Lily!*

"So how long are you in South Pas?" I ask.

"I don't know. My dad might be here awhile, but it's hard staying with him in a trailer. In Sagemont, I do anything I want."

"Anything?" Arielle taunts.

"Sure. My mom just went to Mexico. She's into medicinal herbs—they're cheap down there." He smiles like a boy, very pleased that he has no parents checking on him—and Nikki picks up the ball. "Far out. Total freedom."

"Freedom's lonely," Josh says. "I see it in my old man." Then he winces like he remembered why he was here, and just then, a cell jangles in his pocket. He whips it out. "Excuse me. . . . Yo, Dad? I'm still at the restaurant—they messed up our order. Should be five more minutes."

Over his head, I notice the waiter reappearing

at the pickup counter: he's got a bag of takeout. I signal to Josh—he turns, sees the waiter. "It's ready now. Five minutes."

He folds the phone, puts it back in his pocket.

"You girls can't give up the team." He's amazing, even about this—everyone else treats Andra like such an opportunity, while he says it straight: it's our team, we've got to fight for it! He's got a regular Nokia cell, like mine. I resist grabbing it and putting my number in its memory myself. But I gotta be on the offense now. He's rising, to pick up his food and leave.

"We're gonna be up against a team made of the richest, best-trained girls in school—each one of them can hire a private coach," says Nikki.

Josh is up already. "Get real good, and beat them. You got a minute, Lily? I'd like to ask you something."

Then he leaves for the counter, pulling out his wallet. He peels money out, plunks it on the counter, picks up the food. I run after him like after a loose ball. He opens the restaurant door, holds it for me, and . . . Arielle's behind us in a split second, eyes like saucers.

"What ya doing, Lily?"

"I'll be right back."

She grabs my arm. "I thought no more secrets . . . like the other day with Andra?"

Clever! But I say it firm and hard. "I'll be right back. Let go."

Josh walks out.

I walk out after him. Arielle remains perched on the restaurant's doorstep.

8

The parking lot is packed with cars.

"Your friends are something," Josh mutters.

"They're sixteen."

"How old are you, Lily?"

I giggle. "Sixteen and a half. You?"

"Seventeen."

Senior, I knew it. Cool. "What did you want to tell me?"

"About the guy with the tats. I asked him how he knew your dad—he said he'd been a cop too. He was there the night your dad died." He stops as I take that in. "I didn't know I'd meet you again—I would've asked his name. And I took a card from that place, but I didn't keep it. . . . My dad has another job coming up in San Diego. I'll go with him. If you want, I can look up that guy."

He waits. His eyes take my eyes away—I don't know where they end up. For a second, I'm not in these physical surroundings; maybe I'm inside his eyes.

I slide back out in time to hear him say, "You miss your dad a lot?"

It's like a hit because he says it so simply. But I learned to take those hits.

"Yeah, I do."

"You think people who go are still around?" Josh asks, and doesn't sound stupid. "Like, they arrange coincidences for us?" He waits—I give no indication that this pains me. "I met you on the field, then I went to that tat place—I didn't even want a tat—then that guy showed me the were-girls, talked about your dad. So I decided to get it. And now . . . we're here."

There's a dizzying opening inside me. Cold air is blowing out of it. Then the opening closes. "I don't need to talk to that guy, what for?"

I feel like he wants to say, "It must've been so hard for you." But he says, "Right. Maybe I'll come watch you play. You want to give me your number?" He's a little awkward now, the first time. "You can tell me what came down with the team. . . ."

"Give me your cell," I say. He puts the bag of food down by his feet, hands me his cell. I'm not leaving anything to chance. I click in my number, and my name, and then "save"! Then I hand it back to him.

"You believe in that kind of stuff?" I ask suddenly.

He doesn't ask what kind of stuff. I think he got what I meant. He says, "When Sagemont was all paid up by the government, my dad had a weird job. He was the official observer for paranormal phenomena. He was supposed to document them, and send the proof top-secret to Washington, D.C. Now, I knew what he was paid to do, my mom knew, everyone knew—my dad didn't try to make it a secret, though he was supposed to. . . . I went out with him on those documentation junkets. There was never a meteor shower he didn't tape, or a hail he didn't weigh the ice pellets. . . . When the money for that kind of stuff dried up, he had to look for other work. Mom wanted to leave Sagemont, they argued, she left Dad . . . but those times I went out with him, to look for meteor showers . . . or twinkling stuff in the sky . . . they were the best for me."

I don't know what I hear in his voice. I grip his arm. Then I let go. He picks up his bag of tapas.

"You're an unusual girl."

"Is that a compliment?"

"Yes. Now I've got to get back."

"Where's your dad's trailer?" I fight for any scrap of information.

"Downtown. Maple Street. There used to be a slum there; he's knocking it down, enlarging someone's property."

"Maple Street's my street! Me and my friends walk from Maple to school. It runs across all the way to the other end of downtown." I smile, more coincidence. Besides, I slipped in where I live! "Okay, you got my number, let me know how long you're in town, we could . . . have a Coke."

"All right."

I stand on my toes, try to hit his cheek with my closed lips, panicking that he'll jump back. So I kiss his skin, sort of—I get that swiftest feel of alive and warm, because I barely get close enough with my lips—then I quickly pull back. I rush back to the restaurant door, where Arielle, my schoolmate and friend since we played in the sandbox, crosses her arms over her budding breasts and looks at me stormily, and I realize she stood planted here maybe all the time that I spent with Josh. "You know you really upset Nikki, leaving the table like that?"

"Seems like you left the table too!"

"I thought I'd make you come back faster!"

I hear an engine coming on, sounds like a pickup truck—maybe that's Josh driving his dad's truck—but I don't look.

"So, you hooked up!" Arielle screeches as we both step back into the restaurant and head to our table.

Grazia and Nikki sit with closed expressions while the waitress sets the bill on the table. Grazia pulls a wad of bills in a clip, counts out four ten-dollar bills, a fortune. I'm still going, whispering, but mad as a setting hen. "I didn't! He didn't even touch me."

Arielle's like a lioness deprived of her kill. "But you kissed him!"

"Cheek only! Doesn't count!"

Arielle smolders. "He's your friend with bene-fits. Now he can have you any time he wants."

"He can have what exactly?"

"You told him your sob story out there, about

your dad! As it happens, he already tatted himself with that weregirls thing!" She looks incensed! "What about us? None of us got a chance."

"Arielle hoped she might kiss him. She thinks she kisses better than you, Lily," says Nikki mischievously.

"Lily's never kissed anyone," says Arielle, turning to Nikki. "Nor did you."

"Did you?" snaps Nikki. But Arielle luxuriates in a big grin of confirmation, yes, she hooked up. Just once. We know the details. The guy was no one in particular, and it happened at a spin-the-bottle. But it did happen.

Grazia finds her bearings. "Stop it. He didn't like us; he liked Lily."

"He would've liked me if I had my chance." Arielle snorts, and dashes off out of the restaurant.

We walk home weirdly, Arielle in front, me and Nikki and Grazia behind her. Separated by unseen glass partitions. Then Grazia breaks the glass on her side. "What ya gonna do now, Lily?"

"About this guy?"

"No, about slashing the price of gasoline! What else are we talking about?"

I shrug. "It's his move." I'm so full of it—if he doesn't call, I'll go downtown, check out what slum's getting the wrecking ball, find his contractor dad, then find *him*! Meantime, I have to talk about Josh, to say something about him, anything. "You saw his clothes? A skimpy top, jeans, cheap sandals, and he made it all look like fun!"

"Yeah, he got style to boot. Have his children faster," gripes Arielle.

"I'll do my best!" I snap back.

Scary, a little, how good I feel after one semi-aborted peck on *his* cheek.

But he's my friend with benefits. A warm good feeling, that's benefits.

Way past midnight, at home. I can't sleep.

Meeting Josh neutralized my anger toward Andra. I'm still hurting about what she said about Dad. But it was really the chief and his wife, and Andra told me she didn't care, and they have white-collar criminals over for dinner—a redeeming feature! Anyway, I've decided I'm asking Mom about what happened back then. Everything. Including who's the tat guy from San Diego who was on the force with Dad? A girl has the right to know how and why her father died.

I'm glad I took that piece out of the *Highlights.* As for those starving masses in Darfur, Howard should get his checkbook out for them—the rich should give more. Half of what they got, that would be like, fair, if they want to stay rich and safe. And choose more meaningful causes. Brad Pitt or someone like him is saving tigers, I think. The rich could be saving the melting icecaps, if they put their pocketbooks to it. What are they waiting for?

PART TWO

Like to Like

9

After that wonderful night at Tapas, I crashed into sleep really convinced that Josh would call me first thing in the morning. Expecting to be awakened by my cell ringing, I overslept (Mom on patrol, unavailable to wake me), got up like never before around 11 A.M., and found out that I'd forgotten to recharge my cell. I panic. Oh my God, I'm so late for school, Mom's going to kill me. Then I panic even worse: my phone's been dead for hours—maybe Josh tried to call me?

I lunge to plug it in.

The second I plug it in, it rings.

Nikki says, "We were about to run over. Get your butt to school. The *Highlights* is out."

"So? It's out every Monday."

"Your story, 'Deep Throat,' is still in it!"

"But I talked to the print shop! The manager said he'd take it out!"

"Well, he didn't! Harris came by asking for you. Me and Grazia tried to cover, but he said there's something in that story just like how you write. And it's all over—the students are tearing it!"

I'm gagging. Oh my God! That idiot manager. You can't trust the young, or the old.

Jump time. When I rush into school, lunch break almost, issues of the *Highlights* float everywhere. Goldoni, a tenth-grader who speaks three languages including Italian, brandishes my story to a little crowd, pointing his finger to it. I meet the girls, and they whisk me toward the main office, past some senior guys who are reading the paper. One of them asks loud, "Deep Throat, isn't that a porn thing?"

Huh? What porn thing?

"No, man. It's the code name for that Watergate informant—don't you know your history?"

"I got a D in history."

"Yo, it sucks that Padgett sold out the original team."

"Bull. Andra's old man is giving money. I'd play along."

"Well, I guess I would too, actually."

Sad. But at least my story's successful!

The main office looms ahead. Margie, Padgett's assistant, shoots me a look from her desk, like I'm in deep trouble. Padgett opens the office door, flips her hand at me: *You, inside!* I so don't want Mom to find out about this. Then I get angry at Mom. Look at the injustice her daughter's up against, while she has no idea—which is exactly how I want to keep it. I step inside. Harris's standing by Padgett's desk, with the *Highlights* in his hands. He looks up and says, "Well, Lily?" I get so claustrophobic between Padgett, the American flag, the rhododendron, and Harris, that I gasp, "Anyone could have written that—our team's got a lot of fans!"

"Come on, Lily, it's got your signature." He deploys the paper; words are circled in red—he's been editing it. *"Irregardless!"* he says, as if mentioning irrefutable proof.

"You think I'm the only one who would confuse that stupid word?"

"You're also *the* film buff on my staff—didn't you write a review about Robert Redford's movie on Watergate? Come on, who else would know about that Deep Throat?"

"There are other kids who like old movies. . . ."

Padgett snaps, "Lily, cut it out. You put this in the paper in violation of the paper's protocol. This is a school paper—nothing ever goes into it before it's seen and approved by Mr. Harris, or by me if Mr. Harris is unavailable. You accused me and the school of lack of principles, mercenary decisions, and hiding policy from the students! You also signed with a disgusting pseudonym, Deep Throat. . . ."

"I thought that would be funny. . . ."

But for her, it isn't funny.

Turns out, young Padgett was an activist against the burgeoning porn industry, and there was this classic porn flick *Deep Throat,* which that Watergate informant took his nickname from. I can't even squeeze in that I didn't know about the porn thing, or that I called the print shop and tried to take my story out. Padgett's far too gone.

"I marched against the sexual exploitation of women," she says, "otherwise I was a shy and unassuming girl, like you were, Lily, before this soccer thing went to your head." (Now wait a minute, Ms. Padgett, I *am* shy, but never unassuming, and you fought for a good cause back then, but now you sell out for a gym!) "We're lucky that the city board of education hardly ever reads our school paper—you really made us look bad! But you will write an apology, which will be printed in the next issue. I want that apology on my desk before the day is over."

"And you're off the paper!" says Harris.

Wow, I didn't expect that. My favorite activity. That hurts!

Padgett isn't finished. "And you will say in that apology, you were really so mistaken to be overcome by jealousy and competitiveness, because a new gym would benefit you too. Also, you're ready to try out for Andra's team, if Andra still asks you, because you know that you could learn a lot from her."

"Wait a second." I'm back to boiling with big bubbles. "I will write that I was mistaken to slip that piece in the paper unapproved, and, yes, a new gym will be good for the school. But that I hope to try out for Andra—no way! If Andra forms a team, it may be successful, but it won't have the camaraderie that we had, starting from scratch, building the goalposts ourselves. Those are things that the Weregirls did for our school, and you told me you were thankful that we did them, here in this very office. If you want a solution that the students would appreciate as fair, let Andra form a team, and lead it on the field against my team. If they beat us, that's it—my team dissolves and joins hers. But if we beat them, we form the team, and she tries out for us!"

"No," says Padgett. "That's like the school would be sponsoring a soccer war. Besides, how could you win?"

She says it with such conviction, I'm speechless. I guess I'm not supposed to win! Maybe . . . maybe she knows that Andra will enlist all the big seniors that didn't join the Weregirls, get a super private coach, and in a week of intensive training shape them into a super team. Why not? Money can do it. The little notoriety that I acquired in the last few weeks will be transferred over to the rich girl and turned into major notoriety, with Andra glowing at the inauguration of the new gym— I could never achieve that just by playing soccer well! Or else, the school's not getting its new gym! The matter's been decided!

I shake my head. "Come on, I got pretty low odds. Some of my girls might defect to Andra—I'll be lucky to have enough players to have a full team!"

I think, why does the right to play a final game, to show what we're worth, feel so important even though I know it won't change anything? Or will it, just maybe? I stare down at my old sneakers as if I were praying to them: Can you carry me to a victory, guys, one clear victory, before Andra gets to own the school, the town, the world? We'll walk away from all this without feeling like losers. That's important!

Harris says, "Maybe that's not such a bad solution. If the game is arranged informally, by Lily and Andra, then it would be all right—it's sports spirit, and we don't look bad to the students. In fact that would be a good way to defuse the tension."

The second he says that, I start planning. I'll whip the Weregirls into the fiercest shape ever, practice every day, *twice a day*! If we lose, it won't be for lack of trying.

"What about the apology, Lily?" Padgett straightens a leaf on that rhododendron.

"I'll say I shouldn't have done it. And that we could do with the gym. And I wish Andra luck," I add generously.

Padgett ponders. "Andra's got to be asked about this too." So careful that Andra might feel discounted!

Harris, who is my favorite teacher, and whose favorite editor I've been so far, has calmed now. Now he acts almost friendly, signaling to me with his eyes: *Lily, you're getting off easy.*

"So what about the game?" I press.

"I'll speak to Andra. By the way, Lily, she's got nothing against you. She actually likes you. . . ." I clench my teeth. How would *you* know that, Ms. Padgett? Or have you become such friends that you'll inform her of what was said here after I leave the office? "I've got to go write that thing," I say, and turn to leave.

Behind me, Harris tries a joke. "I'm going to edit it, and my edit will be final. *Irregardless!*"

In five minutes, I write the quickest, most abstract and yet undignified apology; then I hand it to a senior who was assigned issue editor for next week's *Highlights*. Then me and the girls hurry to the caf—we might still catch lunch. As we walk along, Grazia hugs me, and I think, *Forget fairness, Lily. There's always friendship.* Nikki strides on my other side, fuming. "I heard that

Merle said she'll try out for Andra's team, nothing personal."

Merle's one of my best players. Oh well. Nothing personal.

We make it in time to be the last ones in the food line. Just then, Merle walks over. She's a girl I like—she plays well and always speaks her mind. So I brace myself, expecting her to tell me that she's going over to the enemy.

"I heard we're going to play the Barbies," she says with a grin.

"Who said that?"

"Everyone's saying that. It's all over the school."

Trust a school to be the world's best and quickest resonance system!

"Maybe we'll win," says Merle. "Though I heard some of the names that will be on her team, really athletic girls. But don't let that get to you, Lily. We'll play the best we can, give them a nasty show." I'm speechless, so pleased, I glance at Nikki: *See, we shouldn't assume!* We get inside the caf, and I glance to see who else from my team is here—I must ask them if they're in or out.

I fill a plate. I don't really know what I'm heaping up on it. A pair of Pumas step briskly over the caf's floor.

Andra's walking toward the food line. Toward me.

I throw the big ladling spoon back into the mashed potatoes. Nikki and my other friends are behind me. Merle, who just sat down at a table, jumps up and hurries back toward the food line. Several Barbies get up and head for the food line as well, as if stirred by blood about to be spilled. What do they expect, me and Andra will slug it out?

I try to step away—but Andra's in my face.

I look at her, trying to figure the strange effect she has on me. Her prettiness, her confidence, the cheeriness of her eyes—all that should come off as friendly. Like, from a young girl. But it doesn't. She comes off hard. She looks at me with the same manic, single-minded curiosity, and says, "It would've been better if you had said yes to my initial proposal."

Over her shoulder, I spot the table she got up from: all blond girls with that same hard/cheery air.

Andra makes herself smile. "I understand why you wrote that silly piece, but I could've saved you the trouble. No one cares if it's me at the top, or you, or whoever."

I could shove her aside, but just now, I know

this: I must be cooler than her. Even if she loses it. So I reply, soft and icy, "What do you want?"

She notices that other students are watching. "This is between me and Lily," she says loudly, and would you believe it, almost everyone steps away. She has authority! Turning back to me, she says through her pretty teeth, "You're the one who brought it to another level!" Now I hear how angry she is—it's all coiled up in that thin voice of hers. At the same time, there's a lingering surprise in her eyes—she's so not used to being told no. And I've done that, and worse. Which increased her curiosity about me.

"My offer's still open," she says. "Like to like."

I remember she said those words before. "And what does that mean, Andra?"

She giggles. "Good try, like you really don't know. Someone with powers gives powers to someone else. Someone with powers stimulates powers in someone else. It's in the books of magic."

"I don't read books of magic."

"You don't have to. You want to talk without an audience? Let's get out of here." That feverish excitement breaks in her eyes again.

I raise my voice just a little. "I don't have any magic powers, Andra, but if I did, I wouldn't share them with you. You're so pushy and tact-less, even without powers . . ." Nikki is exhaling behind me. Grazia steps forward protectively, the Barbies draw closer too, and it's so quiet in our usually noisy caf that I drop to a whisper. ". . . if you had magic powers, you'd be dangerous. So excuse me for not satisfying your new fad. But if money can buy you a team, why can't it buy you magic powers too? You're not shopping at the right places."

Andra's stunned. Then her cheeriness dims away, like lights turned off behind her skin. She glares, narrow-faced, thin-lipped, not pretty just now: "We'll meet on the field. You get your team; I'll get mine."

"Good. Who told you about the game?"

"Padgett just called me. I didn't know what to say right away. I thought I'd give you another chance . . . but now . . ."

She flips her hand as if saying *forget it,* and strides toward her own table while I ponder this: We mortals are still summoned to the principal's office, but Andra was personally informed by the principal by phone? It can't be. She's lying!

All right. As I sit at my table, Andra sits at her own table, pulls out her cell. I get a brilliant idea—quick, I'll call the office, ask to talk to Padgett, say I'm Andra. Let's see if Padgett takes the call. The truth will come out! I rifle through my bag for my phone, but I left it at home, recharging. Before I can borrow someone else's, Merle and a whole bunch of my players surround my table, talking all at once, all warm spirit. "Hey, Lily, I'm glad you wrote that piece. It got it all out in the open. We're not giving in without a fight! She's amazing, that brat. When do we practice?" Meanwhile, Andra speaks into her cell, nods her head, hangs up.

"Who do you think she talked to?" I ask Nikki.

"Who cares? Let's beat them—that's what counts."

So I don't get to know if that was another craziness, or the normal way for some people: they talk to the authorities, direct. Grazia notices that I don't eat anything. "Hey relax, you taught her a lesson."

But I can't do it. I get up to throw out my lunch just when Andra gets up too. She suddenly sees me before her, and blabs angrily, "Hey, Lily, just because you're the victim, the noble humble one, you think you're better? No one gives! And you were right, I'm not shopping at the right places.

But I'll start. And maybe you'll start hooking up! Loser on that one too. I could give you some tips."

I'm frozen with my lunch tray. The whole caf hears that thin clear voice as it turns into a strident whine. Don't blush, Lily, don't! I urge myself, while everyone turns toward me, girls, boys.

"Virgin-cop-daughter!" Andra cries, like a nasty kid who just figured a new slur. "Virgin-cop-daughter!! Never-hooked up!"

Everyone starts to laugh. I bite my lip. I notice that Arielle smiles—a frozen little smile, from nervousness, I can tell—but I feel betrayed. Fleetingly, I remember Arielle was so bitchy the end of that night at Tapas! I look at Arielle—she gets it and her smile washes off. I can't hear what else Andra says because my mind's so hot with anger, I shove my tray into Andra's chest. She jumps back as it drops to the floor. I storm out of the caf.

I want to run home. Maybe even cry.

10

Our house is an old craftsman from the forties, when they weren't so rare that they'd be treated like museum pieces. The walls sag from all the trees around that press onto the house's foundation.

Trees seem so calm aboveground; but underground, another story—they raid each other with rogue roots, kill each other. Flowers are no different. Up in the garden they're all bright colors and perfume and buzz of pollinating insects, but down below they fight like gangs. That's how you get a whole bunch of daisies together—you never get flowers mixed up, only in gangs. The daisies' gang ran out the peonies, took over their territory.

Roots strangling roots. I hurry home on a hunch-backed sidewalk, with the war of roots under my feet.

I spot Tim's Chevy truck at the curb. I walk up the cracked cement of the driveway and trip on a garden hose pumping water. I hear Mom laughing in the backyard. She's with Tim.

I steal around to the back and let myself in.

In the kitchen, I find evidence of Chinese takeout for two. In the den, two gun belts lie next to each other on the coffee table, with holsters but without the guns. When Tim comes over, he puts his gun in our gun safe—most cops have such safes in their houses; leaving guns out in the open, even unloaded, constitutes endangerment. So he puts his gun in the safe where Dad used to put his gun, next to Mom's, but he leaves his belt just anywhere. I don't know where Dad's gun is; maybe it was found near Dad's body and turned in to the SPPD. Dad would've never left his belt—with mace, bullet pouches, handcuffs, and whistle—on the coffee table, and Mom wouldn't have either. Not when Dad was around. Well, that was then, this is now.

I walk out of the den, through the kitchen, into the backyard.

Mom stands by the unfinished swimming pool. Now she holds that hose with both hands, and it swells and distends like a snake spitting water into the pool. Tim is in the pool in two feet of water. In boxer shorts and a long-sleeved tee, Mossimo, not bad for him. In fact, *I* told mom, after I first met Tim, *He's barely average, but maybe if you took him shopping at Target . . .* And she took him to Target. You can't win.

Tim shoots water from the hose at the dirty pool walls. He sees me and looks like he was very happy just a second before.

Mom wears a bathing suit I haven't seen in years. Her body overruns it a little, attractively though. It's such a shock not to see mom in 911 blue or in sweats. For a second, I stare at her. She smiles self-consciously. "Don't stand glued there— what's the matter?"

"You look good, Mom."

"Oh God. I just dragged this out, to see if it still fits me."

"You do, honest."

"I used to have a body like yours."

It's so unusual for us to pay each other compliments, I bask in the feeling.

I like the tiles on the bottom of the pool, even if

they're drowned in water with dead bugs. Dad and I chose the tiles, white with a blue trim. Tim invaded the project that Dad left for me to finish.

Mom says, "A friend of yours from school dropped by here. Andra Hewlit."

"*What?*"

"Andra Hewlit was here. About an hour ago."

"She's not my friend. You let her in?"

"Why shouldn't I?" Mom moves her unclad legs among the grown grass. The rage I accumulated through the day, topped by this scene of seminude adults dallying around a throbbing hose, makes me rasp, "Did Andra really come here, and you let her in?"

"Yes, Lily. I was in the kitchen, making Tim coffee." A coffee mug is sitting in the grass by the unfinished pool pit. "I heard someone at the door, opened it, and saw this very pretty girl. She told me she was Andra Hewlit, and she was very polite and friendly."

"How did she know our address?"

"Maybe she looked in the phone book?"

Right. We're listed by phone and address. The Willisons, peace officers, the core of uprightness. Everyone can reach us.

"She wanted your cell number." I jump again. "I

didn't give it to her," says my mom—kind of freaked by my reaction, she pulls on the hose. In the pit, the nozzle jerks out of Tim's hands, hits him in the chest. "Marcia, whatcha doing?" he yells.

Mom waves at him to take it easy; she has to deal with the prickly daughter. "Andra left her number for you to call. I wrote it down in the kitchen."

"I'm not calling that idiot scum."

Mom gets quiet, that special peace officer quiet. When cops notice something's out of order, even about their own kids, they stop other activities, and they examine, they assess. Then they inquire, usually softly, but there's always a warning in that softness: sir . . . ma'am . . . kids . . . what's going on here?

"What's going on, Lily? Why are you calling that girl idiot scum?"

"Because she did something awful to me. She really hurt me."

Mom's expression becomes more personal: one party to this assumed conflict is her daughter.

Tim yells again. "Marcia, let go of that hose!" Mom lets it fall on the grass, where it goes nuts, jerking like an anaconda in its death throes.

Tim scales the steps at the pool's shallow end

and shows up whole and soaked. He comes and stands beside Mom. Mom continues. "Andra told me that she asked you some questions about your dad the other day, and maybe she didn't realize that she sounded insensitive, because she never lost anyone. You got uncomfortable, she said. So she wants to apologize to you in person."

I'm dumbstruck. The slyness with which Andra made her case to Mom! The hose is squirming on the grass, like a snake. I step on it to stop it from lashing at Mom's ankles. Andra's a snake. What's she trying to pull?

"Did you ask her how Dad's name came up?"

"No."

"No? Just like that?"

"Your dad was known in the community. Even now, I meet a lot of strangers who heard about him, and they start asking me, how did he die, why?" She talks softly. "For them, it's fascinating. For me it's sad. Whatever that girl meant by asking, she sounded very considerate when she came by, and said she wanted to apologize to you. I didn't want to take it any further."

Tim goes to the water tap and turns it off. The hose, still under my foot, goes limp.

"I'm not calling Andra. Tear up that number."

"Lily. She took the time to drive here; she tried to fix the situation." Cop mode, solving a dispute. She touches my arm now, Mom mode. "Call her and accept her apology. It's easier."

"She lied to you. She did much worse than just a . . . blunder or something. . . ."

"What did she do?" I picture those pretty lips. I hear them chant, *Virgin-cop-daughter! Never-hooked up!* I shake my head so hard it gives me a headache. "Just can't tell you now, just cannot do it, okay?"

"Lily, why are you so angry?"

"Don't hold back because I'm here, Lily," says Tim in that smooth substitute-dad way.

"I don't care if you're here."

"What was the spat, exactly?" he inquires. And I'd like to tell him. Right now, in front of Mom, because to me my mom and dad are a couple who'll never cease being a couple—there, Tim! But I'd have to mention what Chief Noonan said, to Tim, who's a cop. . . . What does Tim know about my dad? What stories are told in the department? *Dad, what did you do? What were you into?*

We're all silent. That unseen wing of fear is so close to me now. . . .

"Can I show you something, Lily?" Tim asks, as if to change the subject. Beckoning for me to follow, he steps into the garage.

The garage is chock-full of Dad and me, and I'm not being symbolic. All sorts of junk of mine, which Mom wanted to throw away, Dad saved in here. Two boxes filled with my old toys, my baby bed's headboard, the Burton tent that Dad and I camped in when we went fishing. (Mom joined us a few times, but didn't like sleeping on the bare ground.) Dad folded the tent and hung it on pegs on the back wall of the garage.

I see Dad's workbench; he'd taken up wood carving. His shelf of tools: hammer, hacksaw, gouge, chisel, plane, rasp, drills . . . He told me their names; I remember them. Wood figurines; a bear and a dog, not great, but for a beginner carver they're okay. And a kit of forensic utensils Dad had never worked with—he wasn't a crime scene analyst but was fascinated by crime-solving. He told me about those too; calipers to measure size, tweezers to pick up fiber, dirt, glass shards. Brushes to dust off prints. A mirror in its plastic case, small, two by five inches. Held near a victim's lips, it will steam up if the victim still breathes. . . .

Tim walks past all that and past Dad's old Toyota. To the shower and sink Dad installed at the back of the garage. No one has used them since Dad died. The sink turned green. There's a tall narrow mirror on the wall beside the shower. The yellow stains around its frame make it look scary, poisoned. The shower stands ghostly behind a plastic curtain that crackles when Tim pulls it aside. Dad put in both hot and cold water, with a grated drain underneath and a lip to prevent the water from spilling on the garage floor. The shower face is round like a clock dial, and pierced like a sieve.

Tim turns the taps on. The shower clears its throat like an old man, but spits not a drop of water. "This shower's all silted up. But if I clean the water line, it'll work like new. Matt did a good job."

I imagine him and Mom mentioning "Matt" casually, in the kitchen, in the den, in the bedroom too perhaps. . . .

"Leave that shower alone. Leave the pool alone too. My dad wanted *me* to finish it."

"But you never have the time."

I didn't hear Mom's bare feet enter the garage. "Tim can finish the pool in a few days, and then we'll all swim," she says.

"But I don't want you and Tim together in Dad's pool!" Then I get tears that I don't want them to see, so I stare hard at the bent shower arm until Mom says, "Go inside, Tim."

Tim nods obediently, walks out of sight.

Mom and I are left to square off. She'll choose a hard tack; I can see it in her face.

"Lily, there are some boarding schools for kids like you. There's one in Oregon, specializing in girls' anger. They claim a ninety-eight percent rate of recovery. It's quite expensive . . ."

I'm breathless. Is she serious? Did she already check on how much it cost?

". . . but you're acting so unhappy lately, if I send you away for a year, maybe you'll miss home, and maybe you'll even miss me . . ."

Her chin shivers. Don't tell me she's going to cry?

"Because I live in fear of your moods, Lily, do you know that? I'm more afraid of your anger and of the guilt you lay on me than of going on patrol. And that's not right, and I'm tired of it."

For a whole minute perhaps, we look at each other, and we both know so well what pain and bitterness abide inside us, we don't need words. We could start gushing out feelings this split second. I could be first: *Is all this my fault?* But I tried that; it leads nowhere. It's not my fault that I couldn't protect Dad. What little girl can do that? And it's not her fault that she didn't take that bullet for Dad. (I fantasized about it: the funeral for Mom, growing up now with Dad, one loss switched for another—sick!) It's not anyone's fault that Mom didn't go nuts after Dad got killed, which she could have, for she worked backup that night—she and other cops were jumping out of their cars when it happened. They saw Dad as he went down. . . . And she didn't leave the force. She had a daughter to raise.

I try another angry attack. "You live in fear of *me,* Mom?"

Let me tell you about my fear, Mom. Let me tell you about dreaming of you sprawled on your stomach in the street, with blood coming out of the back of your head, with your radio trailing on the pavement, dispatcher calls echoing out of it, "Officer down! Officer down!" I had that nightmare every night for two years after Dad died. I had it in my waking hours too. I begged you to quit police work. . . . You told me you couldn't do that. You told me not only that it was the one thing you were good at, but that it was about Dad too. If you quit it would have been like betraying him. But aren't you betraying him now? You don't understand me, Mom. You don't know what I went through for you and because of you. And then you let that brat Andra walk in here and lie to you, because . . . you live in your fantasy of me being a regular girl: hormones, soccer . . . spats with richie-rich schoolmates . . . But I'm not a regular girl. I'm not, and that hurts. . . .

I don't even know what I mean by that. But I feel it: I'm not a regular girl!

I finally stammer, "If you send me away, you'll have more time for Tim."

Then, out of pure curiosity, I add, "Tim's so not like you, Mom. . . . What do you need him for?"

"Because I can't keep living alone, and you're pulling away, Lily, and I'm sad, even though you're at the age when all girls pull away, that's normal. . . ."

Uh-oh, she's putting guilt on me. I'm back full sizzling-hot mad.

"You're the one who pulled away, after Dad died, and then ever since you met this wimp!"

Although, deep down, I know, Mom had it hard. How frightened was she, with me alone in the house, with unknown women, nannies without papers, watching over her baby? Mom had to break the law about the Latin nannies, most of whom had just crawled over the border, scared, confused, but with capable hands and generous bosoms. Their first job in paradise: caring for a skinny gringa kid who cried every night from nightmares about Dad the cop getting killed. . . .

But I survived all that. I grew up.

Mom grabs her chance to push my damp hair off my forehead, and she might follow with a hug, but I jump away, toward the dry shower.

She gets herself together. Her face set, she walks out toward the house. I stare at the back of her body in that bathing suit, find it vulnerable. She's a female. How could she live alone all these years? I don't know. I did it. I'm so alone without Dad!

11

I go out and sit down on the grass by the unfinished pool. Tim reappears in jeans, a camo
hoody, and suede camo shoes. Impressive. He
hunkers down and tells me he's taking Mom to
Simi Valley tonight. A cop friend of his bought a
ranch house in Simi Valley and asked them to a
housewarming party. They'll be back late.

"Look, Lily, your mom could use a little R and
R. I went through a divorce too, and two years
later my son still hated me. I understand."

"If you understand, then you know families
made of crumbs of other families don't work. Besides, my parents didn't get divorced. My dad's
dead—there's a difference."

"Make no mistake," he says, "I like you, Lily. You're a great kid . . . but . . ." But there's something in his smooth eyes that spooks me. I suddenly remember Andra, though, of course, what could be the connection? Then I wonder: did he put that idea about anger school in Mom's head? Anger school . . . Suddenly, I'm so angry.

"Stop talking to me. Or I'll tell Mom that when you're here without her, you watch porn movies on my DVD."

"What?" He chokes, looks so panicked for a second. Did I just guess right?

Tim is muscular, and yet effete. He comes here with a sleepover bag that's always so clean, all zippers and Velcro. Hosing the pool earlier, he looked for a second like a man. Sloppy, careless. Free. Now he's freaked, but he still purrs, "I'm not into that kind of thing, Lily. . . ."

"I don't care. That's what I'll tell Mom, if you don't leave me be."

He bites his lip. I'm a hopeless case.

He goes back in the house. I know he's not going to rag about me to Mom. Maybe he did put that idea in Mom's head, smooth and clean, just like him. Mom's tough as nails—well, most of the time—but that kind of solution is not like her.

They come out of the house together. She wears jeans, a denim blazer with fake sheep fleece inside, and shoes with high heels. Yes. An old pair of shoes that don't go with what else she wears, but I'm kind of mollified—she's wearing them for me, because I told her earlier that she still looks good.

"Where are you going to be, Lily?" Mom asks.

"Where could I be?" I grouch. "Here, or at Arielle's or at Grazia's. You have their numbers."

"Keep your cell with you."

"Yes, Mom." And I remember my cell must be recharged by now. Maybe Josh called. *I love you, Mom. I do. Even though you're driving me crazy, and even though I can't ever tell you anything.*

"Tim, I'll be right with you," Mom says. Tim walks off, down the driveway. Mom faces me, a little off balance on her heels.

"Lily," she says. "Tim thinks we should remodel the house, turn the garage into a guesthouse, increase the value of the property. He said he'll help us with some money, if we decide to do it. Now, I've decided that we'll do it. Look through the garage, take what you want from Dad's things. I'm going to sell the Toyota and all the junk, to help buy a new car. For you, Lily. Your grades are good."

They are, but I never study, I swear. I just listen in class.

"I know we can get you into a good college, so if you want, on your seventeenth birthday you'll have your own new car."

Dumbstruck, I fall from rock-hard hostility to jellified gratitude. "Mom, you're such a schizo! An hour ago you were sending me to Oregon!" Mom frowns. I chicken out again. "Sorry. For real? Where will you get the money?"

"Tim told me about these stolen cars the police find. If no one claims them, they put them on the auction block. Brand new. You can get some amazing cars for very little money."

"*You* would buy a stolen car, Mom?"

"It's not illegal. He used to work car theft—I told him to keep an eye out."

I understand. I'll get a car if I stop making trouble between Mom and Tim.

"Are you going to marry Tim, Mom?"

"I think we'll live together first. That's why it would be good to remodel. Give everybody a little more space." Her laugh is a little strained. "Tim's a good guy. Move on, Lily. There's so little time for you and I to still enjoy each other."

I've got a lump in my throat. I say nothing.

She softens even more. "Go online. Look up some deals on cars, just so we have an idea."

And I sell out completely. "If you don't mind spending the money, Mom . . ."

"I do dangerous work, Lily. I'd like to splurge on you once, before you leave home."

Out in the street, I hear the Chevy's engine come on. Tim honks, quick and light, just like him. Mom smiles.

"I'm going now, honey."

She sashays down the driveway. I hear her open the car door, then a glitch of talk, indistinct. Like: *How'd it go with the terrorist daughter? Easier than you think. Anyone can be bribed.*

They take off.

So now I search the web for *stolen cars, auctioned by police.*

No info. I wonder if the police blocked it.

Search again, for *inexpensive cars, new.* A Mercedes-Benz sports coupe, $24,950, whoa— but how much would it cost on the auction block? I could ask Tim! Let's not get too cocky. **Toyota of Pasadena.** 2004s at rock bottom. buy now and save! Toyota Echo, air, P/S, AM/FM, $10,877. I look at the picture, hate it. It looks like a can opener. Corolla CE, auto, air, CD, $12,277. Sandra Bullock drove it when she played poor. No thanks. Camry, automatic, PW, PL, Tilt, Cruise, CD, $15,777 (only one at this price!). It's still a tin can, and it costs over fifteen! Toyota Scion: We're targeting generation Y, everyone between ages eight and fifteen. They'll soon hound customers in their mothers' wombs. The Scion: a pit bull on wheels, low, squat, boxy, nasty, not bad, $16,000 even. Hmm . . .

I print a whole section of cars for generation Y. I yank them out of the printer and run with them into the garage. I face Dad's old Toyota.

My heart starts pounding. I stare nowhere but at the old car, as if I'm afraid of ghosts lurking. It might have $3,000 in it. Well, maybe only two . . . I try to open the driver's door. The creaking noise of the hinge sears my mind. Like an unseen hand held the door back. I stop, listen to the silence.

I pull at the car door again, but it comes ajar so slowly I give up. Car rigor mortis. But the window is down. I lean in. The front seat is dipped as if Dad and me sat in it yesterday.

Why did you die, Dad? You confused everybody. And why did you and Mom drift apart?

You told me, "The power of love is the power

to overcome differences." Why didn't you overcome your differences?

Anyway, I'm doing okay, Dad. Mom just prom-
ised me my own car—we're selling yours. Don't
be offended. And I learned how to do the bicycle
kick: with my back to the enemy team's goalie, I
swing myself up in the air, kick the ball over my
head with a pedaling motion. Few goalies get over
the surprise fast enough, and . . . the ball's in the
net. But it's so hard to pull off, look, Dad.

Alone in the garage, I leap up into a reduced
bicycle kick, bump into Dad's workbench. His
carving tools and forensic kit fall to the floor. The
kit splits; the tiny forensic mirror in its case slides
out.

I pick up the little mirror. Just to have something that belonged to Dad. I clamp my hand
over it and grip it in my palm.

I remember his voice, telling me he was the
weregirls' "contact," their covert agent.

There's so much you didn't tell me. Who's that
tattoo man from San Diego? Who drew the weregirls pattern in his tattoo book? And who's
Josh? . . . But how would you know. You never
met Josh. . . .

I wish so much that you and I could have one

last talk. What would we say? I'll miss you, take care of yourself. . . . Yeah, you too. And then? End of contact? But if a soul doesn't die, if thinking is what makes up a soul, maybe we could talk thought to thought . . . ?

So let me think of a few things especially for you: I'm this open-minded girl, not too pretty, but I'm fairly tall, and perceptive, quirky, pulsing with life, electrifying for my friends, impossible to ignore—that should make up for the not too pretty. . . . Beautiful, complicated things spark up in my mind, mostly about me, and I'm amazed at how I connect events and feelings from such different realms. How I find the link between them—I learned that from you, Dad. Anyway, my thoughts are my delayed gift to you.

I miss you, Dad. I miss you so much. Someone upset me deeply, by hinting that people distrusted you, and didn't value you. . . . I know it's not true . . . whatever you did . . . but that rubbed an old scab. . . .

I've been scared of you, Dad, because you died. Like, you could be mad at me. . . . That's crazy, I know—no one wanted you alive more than me. . . .

Mom confuses me. She wants us to move on.

Can you move on? Did you already? I wouldn't fault you, even if you are *ethereal*—if you couldn't stand being alone, out there, and got together with other ethereals, that's fine. I know what you're talking about when you're with them. Me. Us. I think Mom's trying to forget you, although she can't do it, but she's trying, and I resent her for that. Even though to be forgetful is human, to be disloyal is human—and I'm human in every way, but in that particular way of leaving you behind, I don't want to be. What shall I do?

I'm sorry I'm getting teary-eyed, Dad, but if I stood here another ten minutes, I could have a loud old bawl, like when I was little. Could you make something happen, to let me know that you're hearing this? Or else, why would we keep loving dead people, if our love was useless to them? Everyone's so hung up on who they lost. . . . It doesn't make sense. . . .

I realize that I'm gripping that little mirror.

And then . . .

Leave that mirror where you found it, Lily, my dad says in my mind. *It's a useless old thing. It's there because I left in a hurry. . . .*

And I reply, in my mind, *Yes, Dad.*

So—one second later, maybe?—I lay the little

mirror on the dusty hood of the Toyota. But then I clamp down and grip the mirror again. Did it throb in my hand, or am I so out of sorts things move by themselves? I don't know. Holding it tight, I sit myself on the dirty hood of the Toyota and enjoy a yummy old cry.

I feel better. That was nice. It eased me. Just in time to get dumbstruck again.

I receive a communication, not in words, but thought to thought. *I'm sorry I haven't told you more about myself. I didn't think it would be necessary. But it's necessary now.*

I'm still sitting on the Toyota's hood, with my tears drying up on my cheeks.

I grit my teeth hard. Then I do something I've never done before: I pinch my arm, tweeze my fingers onto a spot above my wrist, till I make a nice purple bruise—if this is a dream, it comes with all the necessary physical sensations to show that the bruise is real, and I just inflicted it on myself.

Lily . . . Don't be afraid. . . .

I shiver. I could run out of here, lock myself in my bedroom, call Mom. . . . Am I going crazy?

But that voice without words spoken out loud,

just spoken in my mind, continues, and it feels so much like Dad, I shiver and gag as he tells me, *This is not our last contact. We'll be in contact often. I don't want you to be scared of me.*

I think in reply, *I don't want to be either. . . .*

And I spook. I whip around. There's no one behind me. Only the shadow of a tree rising by the side of the house. Dark, richly foliated. Beyond it, the driveway, the street. Across the street, the two-story skeleton of an unfinished construction. The night is thickening the shadows. The street outside, which I've known for years, seems like a corridor lined with leafy monsters, lit by lights marking the direction of an occult pathway . . . leading where?

I don't know. . . .

Where am I now, in some other world?

I think, *Dad . . . if this is really happening, you've been keeping things from me.*

He messages back, *Doesn't every dad? Now, put that mirror where you found it.*

There's something about the little mirror! Or he wouldn't go on, as if to a child: that thing's not for you, it's boring, you wouldn't like it, put it away. So I raise the mirror in its tiny case and snap it open. My dad's protesting. *Lily, what did I just tell you? Stop it. . . .* But I don't listen. The mirror case makes a noise: *ffwaapp,* like a vacuum-packed container when air rushes in. I peer. It's so small, barely wide enough to reflect my eyes. . . . I look at my eyes in the mirror. A kind of animal gracefulness elongates my eye sockets. . . . *Lily, stop that!* But I don't. As if putting my eye against a crack in a wall, I peep *onto the other side. . . .*

12

What I see is a creature that's puppyish and wild. Jumping as if ready to bounce out of the frame.

The creature has such energy, she makes the mirror twitch in my hand—she's about to break the boundaries between her and me!

Here she is, Dad explains. *Your protectress, your animal spirit. The weregirl.*

I'm dizzy. . . .

That's a large *puppy out there!* is my one conscious comment about what I see in the mirror.

Then I try to run out of the garage, but I trip. As I land on the floor, I thrust up my hand with the mirror so it won't break. When I stagger up, the mirror twitches in my hand, or maybe my hand jerks wildly. As scared as I am, I still peek in again: that "she" out there, her eyes glitter with concern. As the mirror stabilizes, or perhaps I get a good grip on it, that puppy frets, relieved that I'm all right.

You didn't show me my weregirl when I was ten, and you're doing it now? Odd timing, Dad.

I stare at the creature, hypnotized. She's pretty! I take a breath.

This isn't so bad. Really, I'm not acting so unhinged. I'm watching (I think) a dream from my childhood, which Dad saved for me.

My weregirl looks like a wolf puppy, but she's a big puppy, and how lovably pretty she is! The hairs on her nose—yeah, she has hairs on her nose—twitch with dewiness, like she just got back from a morning romp, across mists that the sun will burn off, and then that puppy would curl up in the sun and sleep, tucked up in wonderful sierra scrub.

Weak behind my knees, I look in the mirror—one last time, I promise. But then I see my known face. I move the mirror around, to peek on my messy hair, my chin, the top of my sweater. I'm myself.

"Where is she?" I mumble.

You'll see her again.

The mirror looks so ordinary now. Sneaky Dad! What did you hide in the garage?

The mirror's a protection device. It's a moon glass.

In spite of everything, I smile. This is so much like those stories he made up when I was little. The magical animals, the bewitched objects, the points of contact, the portals. So much like my childhood. I sniffle, push back my tears. "A moon glass? What's it good for?"

All kinds of silly things . . . You can use it as a flashlight. . . .

Pronto, the moon glass beams out a shaft of light, illuminating a spot on the ceiling. I move it, the light moves, like a regular flashlight. And then it goes out.

Put it away now.

"What else is it good for? I'll put it away, if you tell me."

It's like being back in time. As a little girl, I had Dad all to myself, and he was a teacher. He explained some things, and withheld others. And I always wanted to know more.

I hear a noise. I jump. Behind me, the shower face starts dripping water. Then it pours. That moron, Tim—he left the faucets open!

The water comes down, gurgling into the grated draining hole. I run to the shower, lunge for the faucets, dip my arms in the flow. Soaked to the elbows, I turn off the taps. But the shower keeps pouring. I tighten the taps till my fingers hurt—the water still pours. This is from Dad. This is a sign, for me! Wishing it to keep pouring, never to stop, I jump in the shower in my clothes and catch a glimpse of myself in the oxidized big mirror next to the shower. The water looks like glowing mist, and I stand in an almost worshipping posture, water bubbling onto my shoulders.

My dad snaps at me to get out of there. But the water burbles his voice.

I grab the taps, and hold them at full.

Inside the contour of my body, the weregirl appears—sleek, sinuously drawn, *sculpted*! A shading of hair begins to creep down the back of my neck. I look at my legs, and I shiver: they're narrowing. Twining with muscles I didn't know I had. A lupine shape stretches in place of me. Stunned, I open my mouth, swallow water. . . . I shake like I'm coming apart.

Then, I crash onto the floor. Did my dad knock me out of the shower? The water stops flowing.

On all fours, I scamper to the garage door and dive outside.

Lily! my dad calls. *Lily!*

I grunt, *Shut up!*

I'm back to being me, a girl. But around the unfinished pool, a flurry of animal shapes crackle with live energy.

The *weregirls* are here: large, eyes twinkling, fangs glittering. . . .

They scrimmage on the unkempt grass. One of them bounces a soccer ball; another one intercepts it; the ball falls in the pool; I hear the thud of the inflated latex—I'd recognize that thud anywhere. Two weregirls dive, bounce the ball back out. Back into the game. Rushing forepaws, head-butting the ball. All the tricks my team does! At the far end of our garden, two acacia trees enclose maybe eight yards of space: a natural goal gate. A goalie were-girl prowls it. The weregirl who plays center mid confidently flips herself up with her back to the goalie, bumps the ball over her head and in between the acacias: the bicycle kick! She is me! The other players yelp cheeringly. I laugh with fits.

Then, like a bystander itching to play, I race into the game. The ball rolls to me. I stop it, do an expert three-touch . . .

And I'm surrounded by them. They jam against my thighs and knees, woofing and yapping, so happy to be with me again. I feel the warmth of their bodies, like a long-awaited family reunion. Above us, the night sky is busy. The moon rises yellow, bumped by heavenly weregirls big as planets. Just like in my father's story. I see the heavenly weregirls, kicking the moon, up in the sky!

I think, I'm going to wake up from this. . . .

But I don't. They make a hellish noise—everyone on our street must be hearing them. I hit their warm bodies with my hands. I clutch fur. A paw steps on my palm, large perfect paw—it can run, hold down prey, dig a lair, even swat a ball!

I manage to think, *Good show, Dad. Now can you do any other magic? Like, get me inside the house in one piece?*

The ball rolls before me. I kick it, then I lunge to the house while the creatures hesitate between me and the ball and choose the ball. I throw myself at the back door. Reflected onto the door, an otherworldly light brings out the cracks in the paint. I feel my father's presence, very close. *Dad, how much does Mom know about these special skills of yours?*

And he replies, *That's a whole other story. . . .*

Anyway . . . how is *Mom? She still talking about me?*

And I'm thinking, You kidding me, Dad? You, the master of magic, you're so naive? Mom's ready to shack up again. She's getting on with her life. . . .

I quash that thought, because I sense that . . . he really didn't know. But then, that might explain a lot of things. . . . Dad was magical, and Mom is not. He was bewitching, and prone to the unexplainable, while Mom . . . is flat! So when he died, they were really cut off from each other. Meanwhile, I rattle the door handle. I can't open the kitchen door.

Step back, he instructs me, from the other world.

I step back.

The kitchen door opens, quiet as if on oiled hinges.

Behind me, the clamor of the otherworldly game recedes . . . echoing lower, lower . . . the light decreases . . . from hallucinatory to just pretty . . .

I peek back: the weregirls, wrapped in that otherworldly light, are chasing the ball back into my dad's garage. The light orbits inside, toward that mirror . . . perhaps, plunging back into it. Then it's sucked in, as if my dad switched it off.

I slam the back door shut. I run to the kitchen sink and put my lips against the water tap. I drink, step back, exhale *haaahh*. . . . My heart stops racing. I turn off the water and walk into the den.

The mirror in the den is the largest in our house. I see myself in it. The regular me, ravaged and soaked. I stagger to the bathroom, pull a towel, wipe my face, dry off my neck and my arms. Then, I tear off my wet clothes. The moon glass slides out of my pocket. I let it lie on the floor. I pull on dry jeans and a sweater. Then I pick up the moon glass and dry it on my sweater.

I sneak a look out the window. The backyard is empty.

Standing in the den, I open the little mirror again. Reflected in it, there are *my* eyes.

But as I stare at them, they change. They grow and their hazel irises turn golden. Like in a hologram in which two visuals superimpose, the weregirl surfaces, overlapping my reflection. She prances in a landscape of brown scrub and watches me with round golden eyes.

I remember Dad's voice whispering to me, when I was a little girl. Telling me bedtime stories with magical animals.

You'll know the good ones, and the evil ones,
*   by the shape of their eyes.*
Round eyes, golden, brown equal magical
*   beings, friends to man.*
Slit eyes, vertical, cracked, equal fiends,
*   monsters, foes to man.*
And there's a third kind—those who don't
*   know what they are.*
Their eyes are flat and murky:
Drab eyes, shallow eyes, foolery and lies. . . .
Malice and evil spell demise. . . .

When I was a little girl and we went to the mall, Dad used to point this and that person out to me—very surreptitiously; he was a master at that. A blink of his left or right eye, with the glance targeting like a bullet. Whether they sold ice cream or movie tickets, or just shared the escalator with us, all of them had to belong to one of the three kinds. Could I guess which kind?

Dad, we had such wonderful times together . . . but that was childhood . . .

Dad is quiet now. Is he sad? Or angry?

The puppy with golden eyes blinks, leans her head this way, that way. . . . She's making nice.

She's telling me she's friendly. She trots off, but glances back. I break a smile.

Weregirl, I call her. *Come to me. . . .*

She instantly bounces back, filling the mirror with her fawn wild body. I snap the mirror shut—as I do so, I hear her whimper like a punished pet.

I open the mirror again. The weregirl lays herself on her belly, her tail by her rounded thigh. She gently hits her tail tip on the ground as if promising, *I'll be patient. . . .*

I close the mirror and lay it on the table.

I try to message. *Did I make you angry, Dad? I didn't mean to mock your power.* I wait. I get nothing.

Then I feel his presence again. I'm so relieved.

I ask him, *How long have you been watching over me, Dad?*

Always. I still am. I took that bullet. That didn't make any difference.

Why didn't you let me know this earlier?

Why burden you? That feels so much like the man I knew, the big powerful man possessed of the most selfless soul. I could cry again, but I hold it in. *Who is the weregirl?*

She's your animal spirit, and your protectress.

Why didn't you show her to me before?

You weren't in danger.

Am I in danger now?

I become frightened. All that maintains this connection are my thoughts, just my thoughts! How can I even be sure that I'm reaching over? But my father communicates. *I'm reading you. Don't worry, I'll help you. I have the power. . . .*

I'm in a daze.

Then I glance at the window to the backyard. It's dark—night fell on the backyard, on our house, on the street outside.

I'm sitting on the couch, waiting for Dad to speak again.

I notice my feet—usually full of bruises and blisters, but now I don't see any blisters. My feet look so lean and clean. I swing one foot up on the couch and examine my toes. All about my feet is so lean and smooth-skinned. . . . Are they still my feet? Didn't they used to look larger, at least one size larger? That's easy to check. . . . I'll try on my sneakers. But then I chicken out. Why check? For now, I'll let my feet look like a photo ad for body lotion! I'm going nuts. . . .

I get up and head into the kitchen. I look at my feet again in the strong bland light of the kitchen—their prettiness doesn't vanish. Then I notice my hands. I bring them up, inspect them. I have terrific hands too! The skin of my fingers is silky. I inspect my wrists, my upper arms. If I look closely, I can see my pores—even the way my pores are joined together is so pretty, lacelike. . . .

I'm me, no doubt. But my skin is . . . resplendent. My freckles haven't vanished, but they lend me character! I notice a wrinkle across the bridge of my nose that I'd hated for the last two grades. Now it's cute. My mouth—I never knew what it lacked to be the mouth I wanted (too big, too small, too smiley?)—is now just *right*. To experiment, I make faces, suck my lips in, grin, purse them out like spitting. Great, in any pose!

I'm attractive! Me, the soccer player, the sweaty tomboy with chapped lips and a scratched nose, the spaz, heavy-stepping except when dribbling the ball. . . . My lips now, well . . . I'm in awe of nature's workmanship, expressed in my lips. I remember myself as . . . pale, wan, gawky, with a bump on my stomach? . . . I peer in the mirror, and get lost in who I am now. I think, I must learn to respect mirrors. They can be full of surprises. Then I think, I need a reality check.

Those two gun belts without guns. They should still be there, on the coffee table.

They're on the coffee table. I touch them, even. They're real.

But then, me too, I'm real. *Dad, did you just change everything I hated about myself?*

He replies, *I didn't. This is how you always look. Your weregirl is working on your mind. You see yourself how we see you. Without confusion, impatience, anger. . . . This is who you really are.*

I cry. I don't feel sad; it's more like relief. When I settle a bit, I think to myself, Is there anything more real than our desire to transform? How sad we would feel, if we lost that desire. . . .

I accept. I look now as I look now. So I ask the next pertinent question. *Dad, what's wrong with Mom and you?*

He's been dead five years, but I still ask that question in the present tense. And what comes through feels painful, a little. *We're too different. Always were.* He says it so simply, I have to accept it. *Oh. Lily, don't tell Mom that you and I are talking. . . .*

I could laugh out loud. *Don't tell Mom? Who can spot a pair of shifty eyes on the street a mile* off? *Maybe she's not magical, but she's a super cop. If you start hovering around here, Dad, you think she won't spot you?*

No, s*he won't, unless you tell her. She's not open that way, Lily. She never was.*

I counter excitedly, *But* I *am open that way?* I *am magical, just like you?*

As if with concern, he replies, *You're at the age when most girls are magical, whether they know it or not. And that's the danger for you, because . . . being my daughter, you're being watched by two kinds of powers; the playful and generous, and the malicious and dark. You could be very valuable to both. But I hope to steer your path so you never delve in what's malicious and dark. . . .*

Huh? All I can manage is, *Gee, Dad, how about the perils of regular puberty?*

Now it feels like he doesn't get it. Magical and all, is he too square? I'd be very pleased. Girls love a square dad to love them, but not guess their whole game—that's the best!

He's going, *I'm trying to be around, to protect you in every possible way. I'm still protecting Mom.*

I freak. *So you still love her?* That's so important to me, I won't even ask other questions, but he messages, *Of course,* so I pop the next question right away. *Are you, like, big in the magical world, Dad?*

I earned my stripes.

So what do you do, every day?

What I did before.

You're still in the police?

A higher police. But I'm not working patrol; I'm teaching.

I'm so excited. *Then will you teach me too?*

He seems a little shy now. I'm surprised. *I will. . . . Anyway, I have good partners, loyal friends, and . . . some enemies. Some other time, I'll tell you more.*

Where's the weregirl, Dad?

She's inside you.

I cringe. *Am I going to be invaded by a hairy quadruped?* Though only minutes ago I thought that puppy was delightfully pretty.

But he says, very gently, *Wish her to reappear.*

So I face the mirror and call out as gently: *Weregirl, come back to me. . . .*

And the weregirl appears in me. The gold of her eyes blends into my eyes; the narrowness of her limbs shapes my limbs. My exquisite feminine look, which I just acquired, grows a layer of beastliness. From just below my surface, the weregirl rises, throbbing with rough energy, and yet . . . she's pretty, wildly, spicily attractive. . . . If I look at her another minute, she'll seem ravishing again. "Who can see her?" I whisper.

My dad whispers back, *You can see her. . . . Talk to her.*

So how do I speak to my animal spirit? *Excuse me . . . hi . . . yo . . . nice to meet you at last?*

I say out loud: "Listen, this improvement of my looks—is it for just tonight? Might it be for longer than that? If it's longer—by the way, I love it— there's a spot on my chin I'd like to change, and a few other changes that I'd like to think about— like, maybe try a couple of new looks, and then decide?"

The big puppy gives me that golden stare. Making me feel that everything is possible, and easy, and magical. I stammer, "If it's to happen again, can you and I, like, do this together?" The puppy seems to agree. She eases down on her haunches and waits.

If you're done with her, wish her away, my father communicates.

My heart pounds hard. I think, *Go now, go away.* And she melts inside me, while my old look soars back to the surface. Still pretty? I touch my stomach. I pull up my sweater, but then I yank it back down—my dad's around. I pat down my sweater, hold my hands over my stomach: I've lost that little gut! I'm nuts!

I still have questions I need to ask. *That girl Andra said awful things about you, Dad. She said the chief said you could have brought down the whole police department. Is that true?*

Stay away from Andra.

Why? I know there are things you're not telling me, Dad. Was what she said true?

All in due time, Lily. For now you better get some rest. You're going to need it.

Wait, if all this is for real, can I tell my friends?

I hear a sigh in my dad's silence. *Lily, be careful what you tell them. There will be a right time to tell them, but for now keep this as our secret.* God, how could he expect me to keep this a secret? *Lily, you must. Trust me, there will be the perfect time to tell them, when they'll all be ready to hear it.*

I still want to ask, *What's like to like?* But I feel that he isn't as close anymore—he's moving away. *You're coming back, right, Dad?*

Sure, he answers. I'm relieved, yet sad at the same time.

So I'm left alone in the house, Dad and Mom's

house, to work this out. Strangely, reality functions: my cell rings. I suddenly remember that it could be Josh and run to grab it. It's Mom. They just got to Simi Valley. Am I alone? Meaning: I'm on strict orders that when she's not here, no friends of the male gender are allowed to step inside the house. Girls, yes, boys no, under any circumstances—I already thought to myself that if Josh calls and wants to drop by, I could meet him out on our porch, or in our backyard. That's not *inside the house,* right? A little white lie: "I'm expecting the girls, Mom. We'll do homework together. Yes, I'm okay, totally safe." In the wackiest way, I really feel safe now. "Have fun at that party. Bye!"

13

I'm amazed at how well and for how long I've
kept the secret from my girlfriends—one whole
night! Arielle called late last night, self-conscious
that she'd acted so out of sync with me, so we had
a one-calorie talk: I told her to relax and that I really needed to sleep. Josh didn't call. Maybe he
will.

It's so strange, I feel like I'm protected now,
even against heartaches of the romantic type. I
don't feel that familiar insecurity—the two crushes
I had before Josh, I used to take out my cell and
stare at it, *Come on, call me, call me, how could
you forget about me?* But not this time.

Josh didn't call. Maybe he won't. I still feel

protected as if the goddess Hopi herself, the peaceful one, were hovering above me. I leave the house to walk to school with plenty of time not to be late. Now, I guess I'm nuts all the way, why not? I feel that my weregirl's walking with me. It may be simply that I lost that fear which I felt every day after Dad died—I'm blessed with protection, and if that protection is a magical animal, or just a state of mind, I'm still grateful. I walk, aware of the trees on the sidewalks—are they inhabited by spirits too, tree spirits, protective and magical, like the animal spirits? I feel memories rising, I used to feel fearful of memories, but not today. Where am I?

I'm at Dad's grave watching people put flowers on his coffin. I notice, again, that man I don't know standing at the back of the mourning crowd. He looks Indian: his long black hair is braided in pigtails. All by himself, behind the turned backs of everyone else, he starts moving in place, slowly. I keep sneaking back glances—he's dancing, all by himself. Then Mom pulls my hand, so I turn and face Chief Noonan again—he's delivering the eulogy.

But I feel that seeing that old man, watching him

dance, is so important. A slow, soundless dance, no singing, no drums. The simplest expression of sad remembrance. Who was that man? What was his connection to my dad?

Back to now. I still feel no fear at all. Before my dad made contact, my life was so full of dark mysteries (why did Dad have to die? what was the point of life?), but now it feels like in the depth of me, light will soon beam. There is so much for me to explore, to discover in life. Maybe life doesn't have to be full of suffering, or maybe I'm just going crazy—I don't care. My dad's watching over me, and nothing could shake that feeling. Not even Andra and her lunatic ideas, although, after last night, maybe her ideas weren't so deranged? But then how would she know? I'll really have to get Dad's opinion on that one!

I get to school. Nikki catches up with me at my locker before homeroom. Essentials first: "Padgett call your mom?" I shake my head. "Good. Andra formed a team and officially challenged us—it's up on the board."

I reply calmly. "Okay."

I can tell Nikki is surprised that I'm so low-key. "That guy called you yet?"

"No. But I feel really great."

She chuckles. "Like by magic, huh?"

I smile. "What else is happening?"

"I guess Padgett's trying to pacify us about the club team thing. Margie tacked on the board an announcement about the result of the game: no matter who wins, the teams merge. Andra will be the new captain, but the Weregirls are all invited to join, no tryout."

"It's okay," I say, trying to keep my peace of mind intact.

"What do you mean—we join her team?"

"I don't know yet," I say, just to see how I feel about that. But no, about that, I'm not peaceful and wise. "Just kidding. If we join, she'll be captain, we'll be reserves. She'll keep us on the bench forever, and maybe trot us out when she needs us to save a game."

"So what do you want to do?"

"Play her team and tear her apart," I say softly. "It's not about who will be the official team, that's already decided. It's about showing everybody what we're worth."

Nikki grins. I can tell she likes this. Rip them apart. Go down blasting with all our guns—that's just like Nikki. "Andra's got some seniors committed to her already, they look like they're twenty-five. But it's okay, we'll still bring them down." She examines me. "Did you do something different to your hair?"

"No. Nothing's different."

She shrugs. "You look real good."

"It's the challenge," I say. "I respond well to challenge."

The rest of the morning and early afternoon fly by. The great feeling that surged through me in the morning never leaves, and it feels like everything around me has changed—the hallways, the kids, school in general. I talk more in my classes than usual. I butter up Mr. Harris at lunch break by dashing off campus and bringing him back a Starbucks coffee—he's a coffee fiend. I run into him as I walk back with it—just by magic. He's so surprised, he takes it from my hand and says nothing, not even "thank you." Good, tomorrow I'll get him another one, then apologize again about publishing that piece.

I compose my lines: *I did something dishonest and not in the spirit of true journalism, and worst of all, I did it to my favorite teacher.* How could he resist that? Then I'll ask him to put me back on the paper. If he hems and haws I'll give it to him straight: Mr. Harris, you know you want me back, and you can talk Padgett into it, you can talk anyone into anything. And that's it, he'll talk to Padgett, she'll relent, because she's so political. It's good for peace in the school.

We'll see about that peace!

At lunch, I go to the caf, find the girls seated at our usual table. I sit next to Nikki. Grazia tells me I look great. I can tell that Arielle still feels self-conscious—she offers me the salad she brought from the co-op—then I notice that her hair is lighter. A born redhead, today she looks almost like a blonde.

I tease her that she looks like a Barbie. She swears it's a coincidence. "I shampooed my hair with this new brand," she explains defensively. But Arielle and I have been friends for so long, I know what I know.

I accept Arielle's salad, eat a tasteless slice of tomato, and listen to the rumors that fly around the caf, because the game is in three days.

Andra's training the Barbies on a field that's been hastily rented, in Glendale, twenty minutes by car. And she's using a professional soccer coach.

Andra already lost her poise during training, and harangued her new team harshly.

During breaks, she pulls out a book, opens it to pages already marked with Post-its—it's a book on magic. She's saying spells, over and over. She's got a heap of other books like that at home, in her bedroom.

And who's the source of these rumors? This time, believe it or not, it's Holden, who was driving that Jag with the windows down and music blaring the other day, into the downtown mall's garage. He saw our teammate Merle, who was going to the video store, and called her by name. They chatted. It turns out Holden knows quite a bit about all of us. Then he dropped all that stuff about Andra because, Merle realized, he was really trying to pump Merle about how many hours of practice we put in, if we were feeling confident, et cetera. Merle was smart—she told him that she would have played for Andra had she not acted like such a snob and did her utmost to destroy the original team!

So we are—as Merle told Holden, so he could tell Andra—pretty damned confident!

The four of us leave the caf, and guess who we

meet in a hallway? Andra! She looks pale and not so well put together. She's carrying her books, like Holden just dropped her to school. When she sees me, she narrows her eyes into blue pinpricks.

Then she walks on, and Grazia says to me, "Lily, Andra really gave you the evil eye."

"So? We'll make her minced meat on the field."

"You really think we're going to win?" asks Arielle.

"Especially if you wash off that Barbie-like shampoo. Practice is at four."

Four P.M., on the field. My confidence is sky-high. I prowl around, feeling that I almost can't contain that magical puppy. *Whoa, baby! I got this nice ball to catch and redirect, so slow down, add your muscles to mine, don't take over.* She's so over-excited. But she's acting well trained too—if I say slow down, she does. *Dad, you are so great. . . .* I'll give you my greatest compliment yet. *From when I was little, until forever, you were and are magical!*

Jump time. This new episode starts with me laughing out loud. We're in the caf again, one day before the game. Tony Meserve comes over to our table to try to razz us. "Nikki, you ready for the game? They won't let you play with your hooks on, you know—no jewelry allowed in play!"

I see Nikki turn just enough to knee him in the groin—she'll just spring from the chair and he'll be writhing on the floor—and then it occurs to me: maybe he really likes her? I get up. "Come here, Tony, sit here. It's kind of hard to kiss Nikki from over there."

"Huh? I don't want to kiss her," he stammers.

"I think you've been thinking about it a while. It's okay. Every other day you come over and say something mean to Nikki. If you want to hook up with her so bad, just ask her. You don't have to play these seventh-grade games anymore."

He's speechless. Then, wonder of wonders, the jock blushes while he looks down to Nikki with a kind of insecure slithering glance, like *What's she thinking of this?* He has no comeback, just sulks off, while Nikki blurts out, "What was that?"

But then she stares after him—he sits down with his friends, still all pink, even his neck is pink. We can see it from here. And Nikki gets a little pink too, which I never saw her do before, but now she blushes, just a little, around her hooks. "From now on, Lily, you let me handle my own affairs!"

"May there be many," says Grazia, and we laugh out loud, and Grazia presses her hand on her chest and says, looking at me, "We *are* going to win."

"We are," Arielle echoes.

"Right on," says Nikki, but has to clear her voice first, because Tony the Aryan Icon has just been asked an embarrassingly pointed question by one of his jock lunch friends. We can tell by the way he shakes his head, moves his hands in the air, and doesn't dare even look back here. So Nikki sees that and gives me a stiff little grin: she's *flattered*! "Maybe I'll take off this hardware, just for the game." Astounding us all completely.

What else is there to say? She's flying. I can tell. I was flying before. I still am. Nikki is too, just now. We all are. Is this it, maybe? This amazing feeling? Like to like?

Jump Time. The Game.

Our team makes it to the field first, in our same scrappy Weregirl T-shirts. Our shorts don't match, but our socks are the same. Andra's team must have gotten ready at Andra's place somewhere, because they're not in the locker room—too good to change with us. Then they show up: marching to the field in single file with Andra leading, her blond hair in a ponytail. Looks weird on her—too simple. Her eyes are screwed in a "stare and destroy" squinch. And they all wear team uniforms, real pro uniforms, all satiny and cool. They carry matching Adidas soccer bags. They really look like high-fashion models on the "Runway" show—today's theme: soccer.

When she sees them, Nikki stops dribbling. "What the hell—"

I cut her off. "Don't worry, it's all show. They still have to kick the ball."

Andra leads them in their warmups, directing them where to pass and shoot on the goal. She *does* look like she knows what she's doing, and when it's her turn she rips it into the goal's upper left corner. Little pretty feet can kick. Nikki and Arielle stare with mouths open.

"So what?" I say. "So she's good. We're good too."

They look at me like, *If you say so.* I bite my lip again. Girls don't worry. Don't you know who else is playing on our team? But suppose I can't get my weregirl to play, or worse, what if she *shows*? I try to contact my dad, without much hope. We talked yesterday, and he said, *Lily, don't ask me to bend the game for you; that's not sports-manlike. Now you know you got your animal spirit in you, and you're so brimming, you'll play like a doped-up racehorse!*

And what will you do, watch from Heaven's bleachers? I pouted, to appeal to his guilt, but he said, *Look, if I'm available, I'll watch. They do call me on unexpected missions sometimes, okay? I got it covered for you. Now go play!*

All right. Just like in the po. When they called Dad, he responded to the call.

And I've got to play now.

Coach Brum blows his whistle and calls the cap-tains to the center of the field for the coin toss. Andra recruited him and Ms. Leaky, the biology teacher, to officiate. Brum'll ref and Leaky'll do the sidelines. Me and Nikki are joined by Andra and a senior girl, Lynn, who looks like a blond version of Wonder Woman. We win the coin toss and choose to have first possession.

"Hope you're happy," Andra says, "because that's all you're going to win, and when its over, you're going to wish you never got up this morn-ing."

"You're talking so much, we'll win by three goals."

"In your dreams," she snarls. Ah, this is such extra luxury, to see that when she's angry she isn't that pretty—but who is, when they're angry?

"All right, that's enough," Brum intervenes. "We're going to have a good, fun, and clean game. Isn't that right, girls?"

"Uh-huh." Andra nods with a sly smile.

Lynn points at Nikki's face. "You took those brackets off?"

"That's right," says Nikki. "You can't play without seeing them on me?" She took off the ones on her face early this morning. She kept some others—I won't even tell you where she has them. She looks better, and I swear, I just saw her check the crowd. I didn't want to ask her the obvious question—*you checking for Tony?*—and get a punch in the ribs.

I checked too. Maybe I'd see Josh in the crowd. I didn't see him.

Andra chooses our side of the field just to give us another little jab, and when she jogs by, she elbows me in ribs.

"Hey Brum, you see that?" shouts Nikki.

"See what?" Brum clears his throat and spits

right by the touchline. Ugghh. Anyway. I know we'll have a dogfight.

We do. Andra's the dirtiest player I ever went up against. She elbows me in the ribs, pulls my jersey, kicks me in the shins. A couple of times she beats me with a good move, but I soon learn her tendency to fake right and go left, so I start to stick to her, and steal the ball right off her. I pass to Nikki by midfield and make a run. Nikki sees me take off, makes a move around one of their players, knocks a long forward pass to me. I pass their defense and steam toward their gate. I stare hard at their goalie: *Baby Barb, you ain't gonna stop this one.* She is some Barb, with her hair set up so neatly, because it's sprayed, it shakes all of a piece! I shoot, *boom,* in the net!

But then Andra starts crying, "Offside, offside! Lily was offside!"

In soccer, a player's offside if she gets a forward pass from a teammate and starts driving the ball with fewer than two opponents between her and the goal line. You can't get past all their players, receive a pass, take it to their goal line, and shoot unimpeded. I had one of their defenders in front of me, another one to my left, and they were converging on me. Then, the one on my left dived forward, level with me *after* I shot the ball. But it went so fast maybe it looked like I had no one between me and the gate. I smashed it in, *goal*! But Andra immediately starts to whine and all the Barbies run from all over the field, clustering around Brum, rolling their eyes, swinging their little fists.

The offside rule is the most hotly divisive reason for which a game might be stopped. Everyone gets worked up. The offsider's always like, *Who, me offside?* Even if he plays soccer for years, he always argues he wasn't offside. The truth is, most times you don't know you are offside. The game's so fast, like the field moves under you, the goalposts move, everything moves, and the ball moves the fastest.

So I'm the same now: I yell, jogging back to Brum. "Me? I wasn't offside, Nancy was right in front of me, between me and the gate. And Lynn was there too."

"No I wasn't," shrieks Lynn, following the script.

"Yes you were," screams Nikki, rushing over and planting herself in front of Lynn. "I kicked the ball. You were ahead of Lily. I saw you!"

"Shut up," says Lynn, and pushes Nikki in the shoulder.

"All right, who else saw it?" asks Brum.

They all start screaming. I saw this, I saw that. Their side, ours.

Andra whines, "Lily plays too hard!"

The Barbies become aggrieved delicate females appealing to Brum's protective gene. A couple of them wring their hands. They roll glances to the onlookers too, damsels in distress. Brum's done. He's helpless against whining beauties.

"Lily, what's with you?" he grunts. As if he's openly blaming me for his weakness.

"I wasn't offside," I say, angry.

"Lynn says you were."

I gather my strength. "Ms. Leaky! Did you see it?"

Ms. Leaky's twenty yards off, on the touchline. She saw it. It's like I'm betting against myself as I try to guess what she'll say—then she says it, exactly. "We can't award this goal."

"But Ms. Leaky, I had two of them in front of me. You saw it!"

It's useless. Andra knows it too. That's why she wanted Brum and Leaky.

I wipe my forehead with the back of my forearm. Andra raises her fingertips to her forehead, sweeps sideways under her tricolor sweat band.

Ladylike, drawing the sweat toward her temples. But then she grabs her shirt and pulls it up to wipe her face: under her shirt, I see her navel, tiny like a raspberry. Showing off for Brum, who glances at her belly just once, darkly, like remembering that he's a tired old bull—I see it all so clearly, and it's such a turnoff. Some boys in the crowd chant, "An-dra, An-dra!"

The Weregirls rush over too. Andra steps aside, making sure that she's completely visible to the crowd, then bends down with her bum up in the air and reties her shoelaces, utterly unnecessarily. Getting maximum result from the male audience: "An-*dra*! An-*dra*!" I think, God, why can't I be like her? Why don't I do the same, right now, stick my rear up in the air? Then Brum blows his whistle, makes the offside call, and takes away the goal. Andra straightens up, smiles.

I grit my teeth and try to contact Dad. But he's off on a mission, I guess, for I get no answer. But my puppy should be with me. *Huh, are you in there? Any way you can help me, without making yourself known to the outside world? Any way you can give me more strength? Please do it!* Then I hear a sound like a little huff inside my eardrum and then a rush of energy fills me up, like a race-car flying zero to sixty in one second.

So you're in there! You heard me!

Now, nothing can stop me, nothing can hinder me from racing with the ball. I dribble, move around a defender, pass the ball beyond their back-line. My heart pounds. My steps dance in acrobatic zigzags, like a native chieftain's, barefoot in the wild grass. My vision tunnels like a laser beam. All I see, all I want, is that ball, round like a full-shaped moon. No one knows my awareness, but I can feel it. Feel it paw and kick at my insides with the might and agility of a wild animal. I run clear into the green grass, into the open space. I'm alone with the ball, on a breakaway, running faster than ever before. I face their goalie. I wind my leg, shoot; the ball whooshes into the net. The crowd explodes.

The Weregirls rush to me immediately. We hug and congratulate each other as we pile back to midfield for the tap. Andra's beside herself and curses at her goalie, screams at everyone on her team. The first half ends with us up one to nil, and I smile sarcastically at Andra when she jogs off the field. She grimaces and gives me the finger.

The second half is a major battle right from the tip. Every play somebody elbows somebody else.

There are at least twelve whistles in the first five minutes. Andra starts to lose it. She can see that her team's struggling against us. My goal galvanizes our team, and we play better than we have all year. I'm about to score again at the edge of their eighteen-yard line, but Andra pulls my hair and I fall back. I lose the ball and Andra kicks it upfield. No whistle blows. I jump up and yell, "Didn't you see that, Brum? What are you, frigging blind?"

"Watch yourself, Lily," he says. "It was a clean play. Don't make me card you."

I'm frustrated. It takes all I have not to really summon my weregirl and chew up Andra all the way back to New York. We hardly get any of the calls. Whenever there's a whistle it's on us. I'm shocked when Brum finally gives us a call, a direct kick, near the corner by their goal. I signal Nikki to run it. When Brum blows the whistle again, Nikki kicks the ball high in the air. Their goalie tries to leap and knock it out of the way, but she just grazes the ball and it spins down on the ground near the front of the net. I run, kick the ball into the net.

I don't exactly know what happens next—all I feel is this searing, slashing pain in my right leg. Andra's cleat digs into the back of my calf, cutting deep. Blood starts to pour out. I feel light-headed and lie on the ground. Nikki screams at Andra, pushes her.

"You did that on purpose, you scum."

"I did not," Andra yells. "I tripped."

Brum pulls them apart. I try to stand up, but can't put any weight on my leg. I have to be helped off the field. Someone from the stands runs and gets the school nurse. "This looks pretty bad," she says, taking off my shoe and peeling down my sock.

When I see the wound—a long bloody mess—I freak out.

"I think you're going to have to go to the emergency room," the nurse says. "This wound's deep. You'll probably need stitches."

Stitches? No thank you. But the sight of my own blood, and so much of it, makes me panic. But I hate even the word "hospital"—makes me think of Dad being shot.

The game stopped, the team's around me. I gasp to Nikki to run the play.

"I think I'd better take her to the hospital," the nurse says again. "If she doesn't get sewn up, it'll take longer to heal and she'll have a big scar." Andra looks over quickly, and she really wanted to hurt me, I can tell. The ball's been left lying; she kicks it just to steam off, into our undefended net. Then she crosses her arms, waits.

Something's going on. I hate that I can't get up just now and swing my foot into her shin, to get her back, like a nasty child. She's bringing out the worst in me. Then I hear a familiar voice in my head. *Don't go to the hospital, Lily.* It's Dad.

I reply, dizzy from the pain, dizzy that he's back in touch, I don't even know if I'm thinking or talking loud. *What do you mean? The nurse says . . .*

Trust me. Tell her to wrap it the best she can, and you'll go home and wait for your Mom to take care of you.

I ask the nurse, "Can you drive me home?" The nurse looks at me like I'm crazy.

Tell her you have a police first-aid kit at home, it will be all right.

I say it. She tries to persuade me to change my mind while she cleans and wraps my leg. Brum blows the whistle, the teams reassemble, and he awards the ball to our team—no other penalty for the Barbies. The nurse helps me hobble toward where her car is, in the faculty lot. As I wince along, I'm busy dumping on my dad. *Where have you been? I've been trying to reach you all day, and this hurts so ba-ad. . . .* Like a little girl who scraped her knee, when Dad comes to pick her up, she starts bawling even louder.

Sshhh, I know. I had some important things to look after. . . .

What could be more important than protecting me? I ask.

I looked up Andra, he says. *There's something about her. . . . You brought up something inside her, when you used your power on the field.*

What? I didn't do anything!

Like to like, he says, silencing me, because I remember the words—Andra said them to me. *One can stir up someone else's powers. You didn't know it, but you stirred her powers.*

She has powers?

I'm indignant. She has *money*! I'm the one who has powers!

It's going to be all right, Lily. Just let the nurse take you home, and we'll talk when we're alone.

14

With her car engine still running, the nurse opens the passenger door in front of my house, then helps me use a set of crutches she brought from her office to hobble to the front door. I thank her, get to the door by myself, walk in on crutches. Inside, I make my way over to the couch and plop right down. The gauze bandage wrapped around my leg is soaked. My leg pulses with pain. I try to lie down, but Dad urges, *Up, Lily. Get up and go into the backyard.*

Dad, my leg hurts. At the emergency room, they'd give me painkillers.

I have something better.

What's better than painkillers? I can't go in the backyard—I barely made it to the couch.

I know you're in pain, Lily, but if you go in the backyard, I'll take care of that wound.

What are you talking about? I cry as I stand up and put weight on my leg.

This is nothing new, Lily. Our ancestors have been using the help of great spirits to heal for thousands of years.

All right, all right. I hobble across the kitchen, pull open the back door, use the crutch end to keep it open. And then . . .

The daze of light I step out into is the one that illuminated the garage when Dad first spoke to me. *Go sit under the tree,* my dad instructs. I grunt in pain, work my way through grass roughed up from when the weregirls scrimmaged the other day. I get to that acacia tree, lean against it, throw the crutches aside. The branches bend down over my face, fracturing the light, as if naturally shading me. *Okay, I'm here. What else?*

Close your eyes.

I close them.

Even behind closed eyelids, I see that the light becomes multicolored—it's like a rainbow light. I can't help it, I crack my eyes open, then stare: it's pouring out of the open garage door! The four puppies come as close to me as they did last time—I could pet them—but they look different. They hold themselves more upright, and . . . seem very feminine. They run around me and the tree, their paws putting footprints on the ravaged ground, until the footprints become a full circle, and he says, *They're building you a medicine wheel!*

A buried memory: Dad's parents used to send me postcards with Native American motifs—I've seen this medicine wheel! The colors seem to rise. Then, spirit beings seem to fill the yard—they move like vapors, coming closer to me. I get a little frightened. I mutter out loud, "Dad, what is this?"

Shhh, he cuts me off. *Magical beings. Be still. Unwrap that bandage.*

I see the weregirls among them. They gather and sit on their little rumps inside that healing ring. As if their presence cues those vapors, now they waft over toward me, and I feel heat on my leg, and a tingling, a buzzing. . . . The pain subsides some, or I'm too stunned to feel it. Suddenly, I see the old man who came to Dad's funeral—he's standing in the middle of that circle, and he's dancing; not gracefully, but slow, limping a little, like an old man. I hear his footsteps: they bang deeply, like a drum, and my dad says right then, *I love you, Lily. Open your eyes.*

But they're open....

Yes, the ones in your face. You know what I mean.

If he means the eyes of my deepest being, this must be my first time looking through them. I see that the weregirls are four beautiful, lupine, feminine animal spirits, but they're human beings at the same time—they look like ... Nikki, Grazia, Arielle, and me! *Like to like,* my dad whispers. And, *link to link,* he adds.

I understand it all. I understand so well that I ask, straight to the point, *But what about Andra? What's she got to do with this?*

You awakened her power, he says.

She's a fake!

No, he says. *She may be a fake about everything else. But not about this.*

But then, everyone has power!

No, Lily ... Remember the stories I used to tell you when you were little?

I remember....

It all comes back to my mind like a jumble of bedside stories. Yes, I remember.... He used to tell me that people are magical, though not all of them. Some are born "flat"—that doesn't make them bad. The magical ones are in search of their power. Some magical people never find out that they are magical; they are so naturally magical, everything they do is sincere and giving and from the heart. But most magical people find that out about themselves—our normal world, intolerant and pedestrian, makes sure to let them know!

Magic is good, but it can also be used to harm and hurt. The unseen magical sphere wraps around the concrete and familiar world, like a beautiful sunset around an ugly urban mall. Up in the magical sphere rules the goddess Hopi, the supreme creator of Heaven and Earth. Heaven and Earth are always in conflict with each other; neither can survive without the other. "Seeds lie in the ground but rain falls from the sky" is an old Indian saying. . . .

As I seem to remember all that, the dancing old man keeps moving inside the medicine wheel. He's shuffling his feet, slowly. I know who he is now. When he smiles, he looks like my dad.

I moan guiltily. *I should've visited your mom and dad while they were alive. . . .*

But now they'll be visiting you, my dad replies,

while that grandfather with braided hair, dark and youthful upon his stooped shoulders, still dances. And as he dances, the pain in my leg fades almost completely.

He was a magical protector, my father. . . . And in his tribe, he was a medicine man.

I say absolutely nothing—I don't breathe a word—because now I know, my father too is a magical protector, and that . . . that's even above the weregirls!

So why don't you take away Andra's powers? I ask, upset beyond reason.

He says, *Would you forget about her?*

And I guess it, from the way he's evading my questions. *She's part of something bigger, and doesn't even know it, right?*

Right, he agrees. *She's so bored, so determined to be above the norm, she'd rather be cursed than ordinary. . . . She would've found this all by herself; you just helped her move a little faster.*

Huh? I sense it—there's so much more to Andra than I know. And I must say, I'm jealous—I would've settled for her being rich, and my being special, but . . . if she's special too, what is she, some born witch?

But my dad is so clever. He says suddenly, *Now, look at your leg, Lily.*

I look at it. Under the bandage, it doesn't appear swollen anymore. The bleeding must have stopped. I tentatively touch the bandage. I feel no pain at all.

I flip out. "This is unbelievable!" I shout out loud.

Stand up.

I stand up and don't feel an ounce of pain.

I can't believe it, Dad, you healed me. This is unbelievable. Thank you, thank you . . . and how could you be so mean, that if you do all this so easily, you didn't help us win that game?

He mutters sweetly, *Stop it. . . .*

I think of my friends. I have to tell them about this.

Not so fast, Lily. You'd better wait until—

Yeah right, Dad. There's no way I'm waiting.

At least keep that bandage on your leg, so no one can see what you got there . . . a scratch. . . .

And I know he's here now, right beside me. I know it so deeply, it hurts.

And what about the game?

You're greedy.

So? I want us to win the game. And I'm your daughter!

Fine.

So, we're gonna win? Dad?

But he's quiet now. I try to raise him again, but he doesn't want to speak to me, though I still feel him hovering over our backyard.

I watch the weregirls get up and trot away, into the garage door. The garage door lowers itself. The magical light vanishes.

Some time has passed. I'm sitting in our hot backyard, late afternoon.

And then my cell rings. I whip it out.

"Nikki?"

"We won!" I have to swing the cell away from my face. Nikki is hollering into it so loud she's blowing my eardrum. She's so excited, I almost cannot make out what she's saying. "We just finished! Merle scored, then I scored, twice in the last ten minutes! It's like we got rockets in our legs all of a sudden. *We won the game!*"

Then, she remembers, "How's that leg of yours?"

"It's a little better."

She yells that they're coming right over, and clicks off.

I put my thumb and index finger onto a spot on my other arm, and squeeze wickedly, till I get another welt the size of a dime. Of course, my dad could make these welts disappear, or not even happen at all. But he lets them form, red, swollen, pulsing, disgusting too, a little, and I know why: they're *the proof* that this is real. This is too good to be true: it *is* real! And we *did* win the game!

15

Later (how much time later? I don't know—I'm about to stop believing in time, or any other tested physical dimensions!), my friends are here. The whole team came to my front door. I walked over, talked to them, we all hugged. I rubbed my bandage a couple of times, though by now it doesn't hurt at all. It's a good excuse—we'll celebrate tomorrow. They all leave, apart from Nikki, Arielle, and Grazia. They're still breathing fire, from winning.

So I tell them it wasn't us this time. It wasn't really us, though we are a good team and we deserved to win. It was my dad.

I tell them the whole story, including everything

that Andra said. I even mention what the chief said about Dad. At the end, I confess a seriously crazy new plan.

"Girls, listen. I'll get my dad to show himself to Mom. If he can make animal spirits play ball in our backyard, he can get down here for a few minutes. I'll get Mom to sit down, and he'll walk in the door, and . . . she'll faint, or cry her eyes out, or they'll slug it out once and for all. It will be wonderful!"

"You sound cracked," says Arielle.

I feel cracked all right.

Nikki's been acting weird for the last half hour. Finally, she says, "Lily, *my dad* never made contact, and he's been dead longer than your dad!"

I can see it in her face, what feelings this brings up in her. I rush to wrap my arms around her. "Maybe my dad can talk to your dad." So we look at each other, both equally crazy, it seems, and hug again.

Meanwhile, Arielle keeps looking around with narrowed eyes. Finally she says, "If your dad's magical, why don't you get him to fix this place?"

To which Grazia counters, dead serious, "He can't work wonders too obviously, don't you realize that? Think of the position he'd put Lily in."

Arielle erupts. "Grazia, how can you believe this? You're a Cath. Your church doesn't approve of the supernatural, or magical or whatever. . . ."

Grazia's right back at her. "Jesus was magical—any Cath knows that—and God's the most supernatural of all. A cousin of mine just took me to this church in Azusa. They're not into the trappings but they're so *devout,* and they say anything can start jumping around if Jesus wants it to. We're thinking of becoming members—our church here is too boring. Anyway, can't you tell that, whatever's happening, Lily's dad has the best intent?"

Wow, she believes me!

"Girls," Grazia says, "Lily went through so much, she deserves her dad to come back and take care of her in any shape or form—that's my thinking on this."

"Of course," Arielle says. "We're dealing with our best friend here, and we know that Lily never lied to us. But, Grazia, if someone handed you some funny little mirror, and told you if you peek in it, you'll see your animal spirit—wouldn't you wonder if you're not insane?" She throws back that brassy hair of hers, which is so blond now I'm beginning to be quite annoyed at her. "My mom would take me to a shrink." She looks around for approval.

Nikki is thinking. Grazia looks away, but I can tell she really liked the notion of my dad's magic reappearance—she doesn't like to see it denied. All right, I guess they need *proof.*

I leave them gawking in the kitchen. I run upstairs to grab the moon glass from my room, where I left it under my bed. When I come back down, my cell rings on the kitchen table. I race to pick it up, but it stops. I grab it, click it, the screen flashes "private number." Josh? I catch myself staring at it and begging, *Ring again!* Angry at myself, I snap the moon glass open, and stick it in Arielle's hand. "Peek in!"

Then I warn my dad, on that private line of ours, *If you make the mirror flat right now, I'll never speak to you again!*

Then I wait.

Arielle brings it so close to her eyes, her eyelashes almost brush the reflecting surface. She distances it, and looks again; then she goes pale. She shivers.

She passes the mirror to Grazia. Grazia takes it, peeks, mouths, "Wow!"

Nikki can't wait. She wrenches it from Grazia

and peeks in too, and then her face softens the way it almost never does. She whispers, "Lily, that's like, me, in there?"

I nod. "Yeah. You, your animal spirit, whatever."

I take the moon glass back from her, peek in, glimpse my own puppy, then I snap the moon glass shut and run to the kitchen, where I drink water directly at the tap.

Then my cell rings. I grab it so urgently, as if a boy's voice (Josh's voice—it's got to be him this time!) could somehow bring my two self-exclusive worlds together and void out all the craziness in between.

Mom says, "You finished with your game? Did you win?"

Aaaghhh . . . "Yes, Mom . . . we actually won."

"Good. Why do you sound so funny?"

"I was actually putting a bandage on my leg. I got bruised, uh . . ." I lower the cell, look around, single out Grazia, mouth: *"Can you handle this?"*

Grazia takes the cell. "Hi, Ms. Willison. Lily got a cut on her leg, nothing serious. . . . No, no, it's not anything serious, she's just putting a bandage on it." She looks at me, mouths back, *"I think you got a problem,"* hands back the cell to me.

"I've been calling your cell, and the land line,"

Mom says. "Why aren't you answering the phone?"

"Mom, Grazia just told you, I got this little cut—"

I didn't hear the house phone ring. I'm not surprised.

But Mom's in her po mode—she wants to know who's at the house with me. I throw my arms up and drop the cell on the floor. Grazia picks it up. "We're just the four of us here, Ms. Willison. We cleaned up after the game, and we're gonna have some pizza," she says in this ten-year-old's voice. "Yeah, we'll have my dad bring some pizza over, and after that we'll watch some TV maybe."

I snatch the phone from her. "We're tired, Mom. We played a great game but now we're beat, and there's no one but us here—you can zoom over in the cruiser and check if you don't believe me!" Finally, I get rid of her.

I think for a minute; then I scowl at Arielle. "You saw what Andra did to me on the field, right?"

"Yeah, I was there."

"You saw the blood and how nasty the cut was, and how the nurse said I needed stitches?"

"Sure I did. You don't have to get all worked up."

I bend down, pull on that bandage, and take it off.

I didn't really know what to expect, but when I see that spot where Andra jagged me with her cleats so nastily, I smile. Dad, Dad . . . He could've turned that tear to nothing at all—well, no! He shrank it, to a scratch that looks healed, but it still shows, like I did get hit. He didn't undo reality; he just healed it.

"Look at this," I moan, and the girls' jaws drop to the floor, and now I'm about to freak out too.

"No way," stammers Arielle, bending down and rubbing her finger over the small threadlike scar.

"Go ahead, touch it, all of you."

So all three of them touch it; then I touch it too—it's got a little scab, and it doesn't hurt at all.

"This is unbelievable," says Arielle.

So. There's nothing else to say until Arielle speaks again, looking at me like I've become a completely different person for her, and she's a little scared of me, but not for long. I can see the wheels of her clever little mind turning.

"How about us?" she asks. "We stuck up for

you so many times, Lily, do we get something out of it? Like, you're gonna keep this power all to yourself now?"

"No," I say, "that's exactly the point. You've been my friends, and my dad wanted me to have you as friends, and we've been doing like to like for each other, all these years—" My cell rings.

I pick up. I'm sure it's Mom again.

"Hey, Lily?"

A guy. I don't recognize the voice.

"It's me, Josh."

I'm silent. "Josh with the tat," he adds.

Then, polite: " 'Scuse me . . . do I have the wrong number?"

I finally unblock. "No, it's me. Hi. *Hi.* What's up?"

Huddling around me, the girls can hear him perfectly. Arielle blinks and rolls her eyes, like, *Why shouldn't everything cool happen to Lily all at once?*

"Not much. . . . I'm in town. . . . You and your friends all right?"

"Huh? Yeah, we're fine. Why?"

"I've been on your street about an hour."

I finally wake up. Jeez. Of all the times he could call me . . .

"I started to walk on Maple, and I called your number but you didn't answer. Then I called information and got your address—you're listed by number and by address—that's pretty unusual. . . ."

"I know; my dad was this old-fashioned cop, available to everyone."

"Well, I got your address, and I looked at the numbers and realized that I was right by your place. Everything okay?"

"Uh, yeah, sure. Why are you asking?"

I'm excited. I wait for his answer with a nice feeling of suspense—meanwhile the girls lean all over me, so I pull away into the den, where I un-expectedly glimpse myself in the big mirror: I'm still in my soccer outfit, but I think that I look stunning. Yeah! I really feel, just now, that I could stop traffic. It's getting to my head. *Stop it!*

I lower the phone, turn to the clinging girls. "Can't you even let me talk to this guy? Back off!"

They pull back, maybe a foot.

Josh keeps talking, and they still can hear him. "Don't get scared. There's a guy watching your place."

I take a breath, *haaahh.* "What?"

"You got an unfinished building across the

road from you? A guy is sitting on top of that building, and he's got a camera trained right at the front of your house." That wing of fear wraps around my throat. "When you didn't answer your phone, I thought about calling the police . . . but I wasn't sure. . . . I'm so glad you finally answered."

"Where are you, Josh?"

"One house up. I ducked behind a tree. I don't think he can see me."

The girls hear Josh loud and clear—I can read it on their faces. Nikki's rather titillated. "Let's go out and see who's out there!" She dashes to the front room, to a window facing the street. Still holding the cell to my ear, I race after her.

We move the shades. We peek across and up, to the roof of that construction.

What I see seems to slam against my eyes: there's a dark ghoul perched right on top. A face like an alien creature's, dark, with a round techno aperture in the middle—then I realize that I am looking at a face with a video camera screwed onto it.

Josh breathes in my ear. "What ya doing?" Worried.

I'm thinking, *Dad, how am I to handle this?*
And I get a message so precise, I stop breathing.
Don't get involved! It'll be handled for you! I'm
dazed. Is he the one who's watching? *Are you up
on that roof, Dad?*

Don't be ridiculous!

I breathe. Then I wonder: did Dad bring Josh
here just now? Josh with the weregirls carved
on his arm? That would be . . . hmm . . . I'm not
sure. I really wouldn't want Dad to be so involved
in everything that's happening to me. Meanwhile,
I can tell from the way Josh is breathing that he's
sweating for me. "What ya doing? Lily, what do
you think, maybe you should call your mom?"

"I'm not a little girl to call my mom." (Got my
dad, thank you!) "By the way, why were you walking to my house?"

Before he can even catch himself: "I wanted to
see you."

"Then give me a few minutes to find out who
that clown is, okay?"

"Yo, yo!" Josh chokes. "Hold up. What if he's
armed?"

Over his voice, Dad signals with otherworldly
precision. *Lily, stay inside. I'm checking this out for*

you. . . . The thought that he's doing that makes me so confident, I try to block off Dad's voice, whispering hotly, "Girls, let's go get that guy."

Nikki's ready. "It's going down, right? It's *starting!*"

Arielle looks scared. "Come on," I tell her. "You want to share in the power! Come on, we're going out the back way!" Arielle takes a breath, starts moving. She's scared but much too curious. As all four of us tear out of the back door, my dad loses it. *"Lily, wait! LILY? Take the moon glass with you!*

It's in my hand already.

16

Four girls stealing out the kitchen door. Across the backyard, frightfully trampled. Through a breach in the fence, past the side of the house, into the street.

Whoever's up there is aiming that camera at the front of the house, but the front door never opens. We dash across the street, around the construction. On one side, a ladder leans against the scaffolding.

Behind us, Josh runs across the street, calling, "Hey, wait up!" He gets to the ladder. I started climbing up already. He pushes the girls aside, scales behind me. "Lily, come back down, *I'll* catch that guy for you."

"Thanks, I'll catch him myself."

Got the moon glass in my hand, got to test my power now!

Behind me the girls start up too, but they're scared. They hiss like cats. "Lily! Let Josh go up first!" Josh puts his feet on the outer ends of the ladder, climbs level with me, so we hop onto the roof together.

We stand on a deck of rough planks. I snap the moon glass open. It beams like a super torch.

I target the intruder. The noise we make, or the beam, makes him spin around, dropping his arm with the camera.

The beam from the moon glass strips his features: a face that's so pale from the blinding light, a balcony of hair, a mouth clammed up in panic. Below the face, I quickly note that he's wearing a light sports jacket and designer jeans. Blinded, he gropes for a pocket, pushes the camera in it. Then he cracks his eyes open.

I start laughing. "Holden?"

Hey, this is getting really fun!

"Hello, Holden, where's Andra?" I ask as I'm looking around on the empty roof, and . . . Andra's not here. I look all around the unfinished roof. She's just not here.

So I turn to the guy. "Aren't you Holden the valet, not like in parking cars?"

"Yess," he gurgles.

"What the hell are you doing, spying on my house?"

"Andra sent me." He bites his lower lip. "Andra's been so overfocused on you, Lily, I wanted to get her some evidence that you're . . . uh . . . for real. You know what I mean?"

Yes, I think I know what he means. He sticks his fists in the pockets of that jacket—I notice it's stylish, with a light frizz of fur on the collar. Holden throws his shoulders back, tries to sound defiant. "You have no right to jump me like this. I could call for help."

"Go ahead." I raise the moon glass at his face. *Do your trick,* I wish silently, and . . .

. . . and the light grows so extreme, Holden runs to the edge of the roof and hangs his face in the darkness, as if in soothing water. Josh lunges, pulls him up, turns him over like a dummy. "Shut that thing off!" Josh calls at me.

I aim the light above Holden's head: it fires the night air. It hits a cloud, way, way up. Could it reveal distant planets, perhaps? I look down into the street. Light comes on in the windows of a house next door to my house. A face pops out of a window—Mr. Robards, a widower who fixes old cars and sells them off his property without a permit. Had we not known him for years, Mom would've busted him.

Nikki grabs Holden's arm. "Come on down, dude," Josh says as he grabs his other arm.

They make him trample to the ladder; they force him to start scaling down, backward. He misses a step. "*Ow!* What the—" We all troop down after them and hop to the ground. Josh is last. He lands face-to-face with me and then stares at me. I pretend I'm not even noticing. But does he think I look different? I'd like him to go nuts about my new confident look, but this is not the time and place, so I turn back to the one we just apprehended.

"Why were you filming my house, Holden?"

"Hu-uh . . . ," he goes, sounding scared and confused.

I say, "Josh, you want to help me? Get that camera out of his pocket."

Josh, his long hair sweeping, plucks the camera from Holden's pocket, lifts it up—a starkly cut, small, expensive camera. Holden growls, "Careful, it's Andra's. . . . Lily, could you and I talk?"

"Sure. Talk already."

Holden looks at me, and hates me to death. "Lily, you don't know what the rich are like." I chortle in agreement. He clears his throat. "I can't go back to Andra empty-handed."

"Tough. Got a better one for me?"

"Yesss . . . Lately, Andra's not tickled by anything—sports, music, guys, pills . . ." Grazia laughs as she usually laughs, a low titter, but Holden turns to her aggressively. "What's to laugh at? I guess I'm overprotective of her, but her parents were never there. She grew up like an orphan—you don't know what that's like." That makes me glare at him so angrily, he's astonished. He can't tell what I'm reacting to.

I snap, "How many people in that house heard Chief Noonan bad-mouth my dad?"

"Huh . . . I don't know, the family . . . What's the difference? Apart from Andra, no one cared." I guess my face muscles move, for Holden freaks. "If you're smart, Lily, Andra could be so good to *you*." He moans, rubbing his palm over his eyes. "My eyes are screwed. I need a doctor. . . . Lily . . . you got access to something incredible, and Andra wants to find something to put her mark on."

"This is not *hers*!"

"But someone has to finance it! I got those

creatures in your backyard on tape." He seems afraid of what he's saying. "Andra smelled something about you, Lily. She wasn't wrong."

I ask through tight teeth, "What else you got on that tape?"

"That weird light . . . the old man dancing . . ."

I'm silent. I try to slow my heartbeat.

Holden seems to regain control over himself. He straightens his collar, combs his fingers through his tall hair. Almost businesslike, he says, "Andra needs to show something to investors. Big business wants to see the proof before they write checks. Lily, if you could make the supernatural available for a business venture . . ."

"Does she want her father in on this?" I ask.

He rushes, "No, no, not her father, neither of her parents. They don't understand her . . . but they won't be a problem. They're off to Switzerland for a week, skiing. But Andra's lawyer can get us tons of investors. I'll call Andra right now, she'll call her lawyer, she'll have him drive over with an agreement. You put a base price on the tape, and on . . ." He points to the moon glass in my hand. "What do you call this witch's laser? No offense." He turns to my friends. "You can negotiate for money, every one of you."

Although astonished, Josh winks at me. "Hey, Lily, maybe this is your lucky break."

"How much?" asks Arielle. Holden shrugs his shoulders. "A million?" she asks.

Holden's parched eyelids blink in contempt. "A million? I know Howard Hewlit. He'll pay many millions to make many more millions. Under a few millions, a new investment is not worth his time."

"Millions." The word entered my mind. Now it runs in my blood. It feels sexy.

"Give me the camera," I say.

Speaking softly, Holden steps closer. "Lily, let me tell you . . . Andra's an unhappy girl. You could make her happy."

"That's not my responsibility."

"You're right." And he rips the camera out of his pocket, then smashes it against the construction wall. It cracks hard; a piece of it breaks off; then it slams down to the ground. Holden lunges to grab my fist, yanks the moon glass out of it. Shocked, I fumble and fall onto my knees. Josh grabs Holden, but Holden hits him in the face. He's got the moon glass in his left hand. He's trying to open it, to flash it at Josh. But his arms jerk up; then the moon glass pries itself from his fingers . . .

. . . and then, suspended in front of Holden's face, the moon glass beams.

I hear myself scream.

A shaggy, snarling animal bristles out of Holden.

The beast has vertical eye slits, with red irises. Its skin is wildly furry and prickly with bumps— like a beast never sighted, not even in a dream.

It stands motionless, stunned by the light, but Holden's clothes move now, shivering as their seams tear through. A dark hairy barreling chest emerges from the jacket. A flash of fangs takes over his face. Suddenly, the moon glass falls to the ground and shuts itself.

What used to be Holden races to the street. Nikki's standing in its path. Terrified, she closes her eyes as it knocks her down.

High above me, like a wanderer among stars, Dad comes through. *Hey, Lily . . . did he have enough . . . ?*

I'm too frightened to think a reply.

Lily . . . ? LILY?

Out in the street, a car exits a parking spot by banging other cars—behind the wheel, I glimpse something still human enough to gun Andra's Jag right past us. I'm already running across the empty street—I want to be at home!—but a cosmic force

stops me and spins me around. *The moon glass!*
Dad signals fiercely. *Pick it up, Lily. It's your protection!*

So I dive and pick it up.

Pale and shaky, Josh picks up the camera's pieces.

Then we all streak to my front door as Dad
keeps signaling; *Get in the house! Quick!* I rattle
the door handle, but I can't open the front door!
Who's with you, Lily? Dad asks.

I reply; *Just my friends, the* weregirls, *remember?* (This could be an inside joke between us
two, but I'm too freaked to laugh now.)

But the door still won't budge. *Who's the boy,
Lily? What are your mom's rules about boys visiting?*
Dad!

But he's adamant. *What are Mom's rules? Boys
don't visit when Mom's not at home, and right now
she's not!*

I'm dying. *Dad, you know how stupid you
sound? We're four big girls here—we could kick a
rapist to death!*

The door swings open with a spooky whoosh it
never made before.

All in!

17

The girls and I file in and the door swings shut. But Dad left Josh outside! *Hey,* I yell at him in my mind, *you've been gone five years, you don't even know what's going on, and you're getting all parental about this one boy? What did you do with Josh?*

Relax, I'll bring him right back. Let's talk first.

I lose it. *You can't pop back in like this and take over, and you're scaring me, and my friends!*

He doesn't answer.

Nikki's bleeding from her nose; Holden hit her in the face when he knocked her down. She dabs at the blood with the back of her hand.

But after what happens next, she forgets about her bleeding nose.

That cosmic light I first saw in the garage starts pouring into the room. Like a photographic over-exposure, it grows brighter, brighter . . . then it stabilizes.

I look around.

Everything's been transfigured. Even the *TV Guide* on the coffee table, the cut-out value coupons to Rite Aid and Savon's next to it, and a stack of bills Mom didn't get around to paying yet (Dad did the bills before)—everything is defined in such fantastic detail, it looks like a wonder of craftsmanship. I can't believe our beat-up chenille couch, it's marvelous! And the pillows on it, of stained old leather, which mom calls "distressed." How could I not appreciate them before?

I gasp. An awakened moth flaps its wings across that light, and its dull colors are just breathtaking. Wherever I look, I see beauty, ingeniousness. Then I'm seized by renewed panic. Oh my God. Now Dad will appear, *ethereal.* And my friends will get lifelong trauma. Now I'm thankful Josh isn't here— boys can't handle this kind of thing.

But he signals, from very close by, *Don't worry, honey. I won't show up. I didn't want my parents to*

show up either, when my friends were around....
And I see the girls bolt. Are they copying this?
Then I realize he really *spoke*! He's talking out
loud, not just to me. *Hi, Nikki ... Arielle ...
Grazia ... Don't be scared.*

I can't even faint. If this gets out at school,
good-bye boys forever! We'll be four old maid
freaks! *Don't do this, Dad!*

Relax, honey, he counters soothingly, this thought
apparently just for me, like on a private line. *Just
once, this is too important. I want your friends to
understand. Relax.*

And I relax, a little.

But when I look around again ... it's a wonder
I'm holding up.

For this is what I see ...

The blood glitters on Nikki's upper lip like fluid
rubies—I've never seen that tint of red before—
and the girls' faces are translucent: yep, they glow
from within. Grazia wipes glossy sweat off her
forehead. I see myself in the mirror—I'm made of
radiant material. I'm light and energy. I crack a
smile and beam even brighter!

Dad comments, *Isn't magic pretty? Why are
people so afraid of it?*

The translucent girls stare at me as if wondering, *How should we behave now?*

So I stare back: *I have no clue!*

I bolt. I hear a drawer being pulled open in the kitchen. Who's in the kitchen?

Then I hear the ice maker spit cubes of ice. . . . Then . . .

Entering from the kitchen, flying at an altitude of about five feet up in the air, ice cubes and a kitchen towel float toward Nikki. That blazing light makes the ice cubes diamantine, and the towel looks like the soul of comforting care. Towel and cubes whirl themselves together into an ice pad, which weaves its air path to Nikki's face so submissively, then pats her upper lip so delicately, I choke.

Nikki bleats feebly, "How are you, Mr. Willison . . . ?"

Good. Nikki, you grew up so much.

"I'm still the runt of the team," cries Nikki.

But you're taller than I ever saw you. (He's so sweet!) *Has it been five years?*

I can't believe Nikki's not crashing to the floor in a faint. Where's my cell, in case I have to call the paramedics? But she's holding up. I grit my teeth. Aaahh, the charm of Dad's voice, I remember how

it bewitched me and my friends . . . and Mom, until the last couple of years of their marriage. Maybe
he put Mom through this glowing translucence
one too many times, made her glow when she was
doing the dishes. Could that sink a marriage?

Arielle stammers, "We got good at soccer, too."

*That's terrific. Thank you for what great friends
you've been to Lily.*

Even a ghost, if it expresses heartfelt feelings,
will get to a girl's heart. My friends react so
moved! Nikki raises her hand to check the ice
soothing her upper lip—the ice is maintaining its
altitude by itself.

Mhm, says my dad, soft like when he talked to
the four little Weregirls after kicking that childhood ball. *Sorry about what just happened. You
went out to scare off a clown and he proved to be
more than that. . . . but I'll take care of it. . . .*

I dare to ask, "Dad, is Holden going to look
like that from now on?"

*Not when he drops Andra off to school. You just
saw him through your weregirl's eyes—that's what
he looks like deep inside. I told you about how the
law of magic called like to like. You have powers,
you can draw out the powers in someone else—but
not everyone's power is pretty to see.*

Meantime, the four of us glance at each other: *So, we have powers!*

The moon glass did its job, he adds jovially. I can tell he's not quite sure, should he treat us like children, and this like a fairy story? *It's one of our simplest tools. We have others that are more sophisticated. . . . Girls, each one of you is protected by her weregirl. Each one of you has your own weregirl helping you. Now, I'm about to be called to an emergency. So listen carefully. . . .*

I already know what Dad will say.

Everyone wants magic in their lives. All people crave magic in their lives, yet they're afraid of it. So most of them never let go and enjoy it.

What do you think, Grazia? he asks suddenly. *What is just like magic?*

"Uh . . . dreams?" Grazia tries.

Right. All people are aware of magic in their dreams. They remember their dreams, speak about them, are not afraid that their oddest dreams could make them seem like freaks.

But when they get a chance to share in real magic, here and now, even in order to do good—they're terrified. They run away, and seek refuge in stupidity, routine, envy, fear.

That's why children are magical, because they don't know the rules.

That's why poets are mistaken for madmen, because they keep refusing to learn the rules.

At the core of anything good, there is a piece of magic.

At the core of anything kind, there is a piece of magic.

And most times, at the core of anything ambitious and greedy, there is a piece of witchery.

He pauses. I've so enjoyed his voice in the last few minutes, my heart is tearing up. In a few minutes, he will have to go away—what will I be left with? Better ask him, right now, for some practicable magic skills, and extraordinary abilities, and reliable tricks.

I wanted to hold back on something, Lily, but there have been some events that I didn't expect, so I'll reveal this to you earlier than I wanted. Magic has two sides: beauty, and power. I'll let you and your friends have as much beauty as you like, your own, the world's . . . But I'd rather not give you your power yet. For now. Power is a burdensome gift.

Wait a second! Whispering, stammering, brushing our glowing hair behind our ears, huddling together though we don't know where exactly to face, but we stand so united, we're all asking for the same thing. "Give us our powers. We're not little girls anymore, thank you."

"I don't dig prettiness," says Arielle. "Power, that'd be something."

I'm telling you for your own good: there's only trouble in power!

Really? I ask. *How about your power, Dad? Why don't you give up your power?*

That conceited Andra claims she's interested in magic, he answers, *but all she craves is power. Stay away from her. She's more than you think. If some vile breed, some agency of evil chooses her to battle its way back here, that's a job for me, not for you.*

"That's because you don't trust us with power," says Nikki.

It's too much, all of a sudden, he answers. Jeez, this is like, you can't drive a car by yourself before you're sixteen, that's the rules!

Lily, help me here. I'm sorry I was an unusual dad. I'm like all dads when I want you to get easily what I had to fight for.

I get emotional. "Dad, you weren't unusual, you were good. Anyway, if you can't give us like major power now . . . at least, *some* power . . ."

All right, you keep the moon glass. And call the

weregirls when you need help. Just like I showed you, Lily, go inside yourself. Your protectors are in there. On occasion, they'll need your help. Ride with them. You'll have such fun. You'll share the most wonderful ride. . . .

I look around the room, read the girls' faces. Oh well, if we can't get more just now . . .

Grazia asks eagerly, "So, we're trainees?"

Dad laughs. *Tough bargainer, Grazia. I didn't suspect it of you.*

Yes . . . Apart from the like to like, there's another law called the link to link. Always know who's your upper link, and who's your lower. You report to your team captain, and she reports to me. Lily, don't let me catch you offside.

I don't like the reporting part, but I'll be sure to make it adjustable. Like in the field: Me offside, Coach? Not me, ever! I can tell the girls are excited, though Nikki shoots me a glance like, *Could we have done better?*

My dad's finding it hard to leave us. *Magic's unusual,* he mutters, *but it's my experience, if people share in magic, they're never sorry they did. Remember how I sang to you, Lily?*

He used to sing to me, and to us. He hummed even-toned, like men do:

Round eyes, golden, brown equal magical
*   beings, friends to man. . . .*
Slit eyes, vertical, cracked equal fiends,
*   monsters , foes to man. . . .*
And there's the third kind, the trickiest of all,
Those who can swing whichever way,
the way the wind blows, and the freshest
*   blood flows,*
making innocents suffer through tortures and
*   throes,*
Their eyes are flat and murky,
Drab eyes, shallow eyes, foolery and lies,
Malice and evil spell demise. . . .

He stops singing. *I'll see you, Weregirls.* But then, as if reluctant to go, he adds, *Now that you know so much already . . . hear this too: there's more spirits up here than the whole Earth population, a thousandfold, good, bad . . . The force I'm part of has its hands full, and that old war between good and bad is still being fought. Whatever you call it, God versus Satan, Christ versus anti-Christ, Magic versus Witchery, Good versus Evil, it's the same war—*

I cut him off, out loud. "Why is evil always winning the war, Dad, why?"

He replies very softly, *It's not winning. It just seems that way.*

"Then it should've been defeated already!"

If no evil existed in the world, humans wouldn't appreciate the good. They wouldn't be able to make moral choices. I should've taught you the philosophy of our tribes. It's not too late. Anyway, you get busy with your magical age, and I with winning that war. . . . Slowly but surely . . .

I love to hear that: the death of my dad the hero was not wasted. So I ask, "You having fun? Bigger responsibilities than with the staid old SPPD?"

Yeah. I get to train field commanders.

"Let me help you win your war!"

No, honey . . . just because the good always wins in the end—at least it did so far. But I want you to have the greatest fun ride—it's what I didn't have, and I'll see that you have it without peril.

All right. Then do something fun now, I say.

There's a faint noise as the moon glass, which was left lying on the table, gyrates and sits up on its narrow side.

Then it flips open and turns on the TV!

A late-night movie, one of our favorite oldies, *Terminator.* Me and the girls love its low-budget look. John Conner's mother's home could've been one of ours. On the screen, Kyle Reese just rushed back from the future to protect Sarah Conner, but Kyle's a wolf creature now—shaggy all over, uncontrollably hairy—and Sarah is sexily downy, all over. Every human in the cast is some kind of animal, except for Arnold, who looks exactly like when we saw the movie last. He's that cyborg in human skin, blasts adversaries in half, *hasta la vista,* baby! All of four of us laugh. Arnold couldn't possibly need a protecting animal, because he's a machine! Funny, Dad! I laugh till I cry. *Dad, you were never evil, were you?*

No, Lily. Not ever. And I enjoyed my ride though it was short, but yours will be longer and more fun. Yours will be the best, Lily.

And that's it. His voice fades, that magical light vanishes, and me and my friends don't glow anymore.

18

I hear someone knocking at the back door. I open the door and Josh peers in, that smashed camera still in his hand. Arielle flips back her hair and grins enticingly. But Josh stares only at me. "You okay?"

I nod.

He hesitates, steps in. "You didn't have to lock the door, you know."

"I'm sorry. I don't know why I did that. . . ."

Josh is shaking. His whole body is on extreme alert. He combs his hair back twice in succession and stutters, "Lily, my dad . . . never saw anything paranormal . . . never taped anything weird, not even crazy lights in the desert . . . but the stuff that guy was filming, it was paranormal, wasn't it?"

He puts the camera on the kitchen table, in three pieces. "Maybe we can find a store to fix this, and see what he taped. . . . If it's all right with you. . . ."

"Take it easy," I say. "Things are under control."

"Are they? Lily, if you're in trouble, anything I can do . . ."

Chivalrous enough. Good sign.

"It's all right, Josh," says Arielle, stepping forward and twirling a piece of her hair. "We're all right. We've put up with this before."

That's it. I have to get him out of here. I talk very fast. "So I guess you were ready to get going. Let me walk you out."

I push him out the back door; then I shoot the girls a hard stare: *Stay in the kitchen, and don't budge! Remember link to link? I'm your captain, the top link. You listen to me!* Then I slam the door unnecessarily hard.

I shake my head.

"You know, you look so great . . ."

Huh?

That was Josh. Standing in my ravaged backyard, not knowing what to do, confused and overpowered, under the ordinary night sky.

Ah, at last! A direct compliment.

But guess what? To take compliments . . . it's awkward, kind of. I'm not used to it. So I think of a million clever things to say back, and choose just one. "Thanks," I breathe.

Then I babble, "You don't think I'm a mess?"

"You? Nah." Josh's voice gets throaty. "Hell no, you're *pretty*. Lily . . . what's going on?"

Be careful what you tell him! my dad interjects so brusquely, like he's inside my brain.

I thought you were leaving, Dad!

I was. But you don't know who this guy is.

I know a good deal more who he is than you do. He's a boy who likes me!

We all got that. But if he's not magical—and he's not—you're wasting your time. It won't work. Even Mom and I couldn't breach that difference in the end.

Even Mom and I! *Well, there's no reason why I shouldn't handle difference better than both of you together.* Yet I notice that I'm already pacing away from Josh. Dad has such influence over me. Just leave now, will you, Dad?

Magic and no magic don't mix. He's not magic. Of course, it's not his fault.

So what, I'm not getting married. Dad, what are

you trying to pull with that? You're sabotaging me from hooking up! Go away, or if you don't . . . at least shut up!

"So," says Josh, "I guess I'm heading out now. . . ."

He hesitates, then reaches in a back pocket of his large and comfy cargo pants. He pulls a small book with a dark cover out of it.

"I thought you might be interested in reading this."

I take the book. It feels very dry and hard, very impersonal. I don't like old books—they're not nice to snuggle into bed with, and when I read them, I can't dogear their pages; they fritter. So I've not wasted time on an old book since some required reading in eighth grade. I open this one with the same distaste. The title's written in skinny fonts:

Cases Suggestive of Animal Transformation among the Tribal Navajos.

I look at the back of the dust jacket: a photo showing a square guy with glasses. The blurb underneath explains that he's a psychologist specializing in Native American tribes.

"I thought you'd be interested," Josh mutters. Then he lowers his voice. "I know what's different about you, Lily. Your hair. I didn't realize last time how pretty it is."

"You only saw me two times before," I reply to Josh.

"Three. One game, two at that restaurant, three tonight."

And he's the one who said it!

"I'm the same as always," I say, dying of candidness. At the same time, it crosses my mind that maybe I should get on long distance with Dad, to ask him a very tiny favor: could he get those girls off me for *one second*? I feel the vibration of their curiosity through the house's back door—they'll break that old door by leaning into it, to eavesdrop. Then I think Dad might do some funny trick and spook this guy even worse. Forget about asking him anything—I'll take the circumstances as they are.

"I'm a very normal girl," I declare. "I'm a totally ordinary girl."

"Yeah," he grunts. "A little too hung up on your wizard dad—other than that . . ."

"Last time we talked, you thought my wizard dad was cool."

"Sure. But when you get to face wizardry close up, it's different."

We stand in the backyard. I've never looked better and never felt less sure of myself. So I pace my heartbeat, and think, Lily, just enjoy this guy. Then I remember Dad saying that Josh isn't magical, that it won't work. What should I do?

"My dad thinks we're not for each other . . . you know . . . ?" Maybe being honest is the best weapon.

Josh is silent. Defensive. "He knows nothing about me. What do you think?"

"I don't know," I say truthfully.

"Well, shouldn't we find out for ourselves?"

I laugh. He laughs too. Then he says, as if moving to safer ground, "Too bad my dad never met your dad. They might've gotten along."

"Yeah . . . What's with us and our dads, Josh?"

"We didn't know we loved them so much."

Hey, hey. He's like, being very deep right now.

"Josh. You want to sit with me a minute?"

I dash to the side of the garage. There's a lot of old junk heaped up against it. I rummage for an old rubber mattress, drag it out near the edge of the pool. I spread the mattress, sit down first, bring my knees up.

"When we saw each other last," he says, lowering himself next to me, "I figured you were kind of like me. I know something about growing up odd, without many friends . . . so maybe you'd like to talk to me. But then I come here, you got a whole crowd of friends, your dad, magical tools . . . What the hell would you need me for?"

"I see. If you're not the hero, it's not worth it to you?"

He gets irritated. "I wanted to help you. But you're handling it."

Then he slumps onto the mattress, and we touch shoulders. He doesn't pull back.

I say nothing for almost a whole minute. Then I whisper, "Don't say that just to say it. I might believe you."

"Believe me," he growls. "Day after we met at that restaurant, I borrowed my dad's truck and drove down to San Diego. I looked for that tat shop. I found it locked up, with an eviction notice on the door. When I asked about the guy at a burrito place across the road, everyone was like, 'What guy?' Like he'd never been there. Isn't that crazy?"

I shrug. "Much crazier stuff's happening."

Then I wait. But nothing happens.

I think hard. *Dad? Just go away, okay? You're inhibiting this kid!*

And I suddenly get this sense of no magical

presence. Just the reality, narrow and flat. The trees and grass and stars and high wispy clouds lose their gloss of wondrousness, and the rubber mattress under me feels as unromantic as it truly is—a sun-drenched, half-melted, old, dusty piece of rubber.

In that suddenly impoverished landscape, Josh puts his hands on my waist. I jolt. I look him in the face. He pulls his hands back.

I mutter, "It's all right, Josh. I'm cool."

The nerve of me! But he isn't doing anything now. So how can I encourage him without acting like a slut?

I put my hands on Josh's cheeks. Keeping my lips shut tightly, I move closer, but then I stop. He's shy too, I can tell. He's sitting so still! What would Dad say about Josh now? Then I think, The hell with Dad's warning. And I move in to kiss him, but it's too late—I can tell that the moment passed. He's way too self-conscious. Then I stand up.

"All right," he says, standing up too. "You need anything, you call me. Huh?"

I'm quiet.

"You don't want this book? I got it for you."

"*I'm* the book," I reply, before I even think of what I'm saying. Staring at him. Then he opens the book, tears out an end page—it's got something scribbled on it. "I wrote my number down," he says. "Call me and let me know when your next game is. Or . . . just call me. . . ."

And then I think, we hooked up. We did. Doesn't have to be lips and tongue, the very first time! Meanwhile, I say out loud, "I don't know when our next game will be. We beat the Barbies. I wonder what Ms. Padgett will do now, to merge my team with Andra's."

"Don't merge it," he says. "Keep yours a club team. At least it will be yours."

"Yeah, I guess we'll settle to be just a club team."

He smiles, turns, and walks down the driveway. I bounce after him while he strides toward the sidewalk bucked up by the roots of the trees at war—and I jump, and the hair on the back of my neck pricks up like bits of wire. There is a man at the end of the driveway. He's old; his face looks like tree bark broken by knots. . . . His eyes are dead black embers. . . . And then I recognize him. "Mr. Robards, you can't sneak up on me like that."

"What's going on here?" slurs our neighbor who sells cars illegally. "I saw this tremendous light coming out of your garage. Then it moved across the street. I saw it up there." He points to the top of that building across from us.

"I don't know what you saw. I blew a fuse in my dad's garage earlier. . . ."

"Fuses don't make that kind of glare!" He starts walking up the driveway. "What's going on?"

"Nothing, Mr. Robards. I don't know what you saw. Please don't march in here—you're trespassing!"

My tone clues him in: I won't let him advance farther. He growls, "Why isn't your mother ever here?" Then he starts backing out while I stare at him, and that look of unkempt bark with knots comes over his face again and vanishes as swiftly, but I do see it. He huffs back, but when he gets in the street he stares long and hard at the roof across the way. But now the roof is empty, and utterly in the dark.

"That guy's going to make trouble," says Josh.

"Never mind him. You going to call me soon?"

"Yes. I'll help my dad on that job he got downtown. I'll stick around awhile." He smiles and walks off.

I glance right and left. The street seems deserted. The darkness is cold, but it doesn't feel unsafe. I pace across our backyard and find the back door open a crack, with a watchful little eye framed in it. I yank the door open, thinking *I'm going to kill you, Arielle!* But it's Nikki this time, who says, "You didn't kiss him," in a tone of honest disappointment.

"I would have," I say, trying to sound angry, "if you guys didn't interfere like, every second. He totally saw you peeking and got nervous and bailed."

"He didn't see me! You didn't either!"

"I knew someone was peeking. I was so close."

"Sucks having your luck." Arielle snickers.

I shrug. I notice that Nikki changed clothes. "Hey, that's my shirt, isn't it?"

"Yes," she says, "and your other training pants. I got that nosebleed all over my things."

I laugh. "Come on, let's raid my mom's closet and see if we can come up with some really cool outfits."

"Your mom, low odds," rags Arielle, but we all race up the stairs, yelling, "Fashion show!"

I guess we needed to do something fun and mindless to feel normal again. My mom has a box of costume jewelry from when she and my dad went out, once in a blue moon. I dump it on the floor in my room. We dive right in, draping fake pearls around our necks, wrapping scarves, clinging bracelets. One brand of knockoffs after another, but we manage to put together some getups. Grazia and Arielle use a whole can of hairspray to tease their hair like rocker chicks. Nikki turns on MTV, grabs a curling iron, holds it as a mike, calling our names one by one to walk down the hallway, like it's a runway. She announces the scene, speaking in French, she says— I can't tell. We go back down, get Nikki's clothes washed and hung, turn MTV back on, and dance and sing into the handles of hairbrushes. We laugh and scream. Dad pledged us his magic protection. Nothing bad can happen to us. . . .

Everyone is passed out, except for me. Nikki and Arielle sleep head to toes in my bed, and Grazia snores on the couch in the den.

That's how I feel too: drained. I think of Josh. I realize I'm not at all nervous about being alone with him next time, which is a totally new feeling for me. Boys always made me nervous, but no more! I give a thought to getting my log and jotting this in—this is important enough to be memorialized. But I'm so beat, my eyes are blurring. Another time . . . I can barely make it to my bedroom, where I lie on the floor next to my already occupied bed, and . . .

I'm jolted awake by Nikki, who is shaking me by my shoulder.

The bedroom is still dark, but the alarm clock reads 6:14.

"I need some clothes from you, Lily," Nikki whispers.

I mumble through glued-up lips, "Yours must be dry by now."

"I can't wear my clothes; they shrunk. Or I got taller."

"Hunhhh?"

She grabs me, pulls me up.

Nikki's crying. I get so scared, my heart jumps up into my throat.

Then I realize . . . Nikki . . . seems taller.

Nikki's barely five feet. But just now, I'm dreaming, or *I* shrunk, or she *is* taller! She stands in front of me, in a T-shirt and old pajama pants of mine. Tears draw shiny paths on her cheeks. She throws her arms around me, her hug matching my height.

I can't take this.

I feel like diving back into my bed, piling the pillows over my face, sinking, and waking up again. To a regular day. But then . . .

I remember. Everything. So I bust the bathroom door open, shove Nikki into the bathroom, and stand next to her, both facing the nearest large mirror. My heart's pounding like a hurricane. I'm still me, but with a well-proportioned chin, an elegantly narrowed face, and lips marvelously arched and full, not too much, not too little! Just right. As for Nikki, she's . . . the same, well almost! I hug her, finding her face strangely elevated next to mine, and I whisper, trying to believe what I'm saying, or I'll go crazy: "You're not slouching anymore, that's all."

"No, no, look! I *am* taller!"

She was always the smallest of us. Dad used to joke with her: *Hey, Nikki, did you know the greatest boxing champions are always featherweights?* But he joked with her because it was so obvious she suffered from being short. Now, I don't know what it is—is she just holding herself in a completely different way? She babbles, "I just tried my pants—they stop way above my ankles. What will the kids say at school?"

"Maybe they won't notice. Don't worry. Let's get you some clothes."

It's probably the truth, most kids are so selfishly into themselves.

"Where's that little mirror? Give it to me."

Where did I leave it? Then I remember that I put it on my bedside table.

I grab it, give it to Nikki, who grins. "I want to see what I look like." She sounds just crazy.

She opens the case, looks at herself, and acts even more crazy. "There's my weregirl in there," she breathes to me. "Hey, weregirl," she coos at that slit-shaped portal. The irises of her eyes move, as if following the movement of a bouncy, nimble creature. "I look just like you, you know?" I never heard Nikki be goony like that before.

She holds up the mirror case. "Wanna look?"

"Sure . . ."

I peer in there.

I guess this is Nikki's weregirl. This one prances on long thin muscled legs, she's darker than *my* weregirl, and she has a kind of urchin look—but attractive, sexy actually in a way that hasn't quite filled in, and smart movements, a kind of dribbling quickness. She's Nikki, all right.

Nikki says, "Because your dad did this . . . I really feel like I'm your sister."

I don't know what to answer. I'm choked up.

"Come on, Sister," I say. "Let's put some clothes on you."

Of course, sisters are a pain in the butt. I have one good pair of sweatpants—those are the only ones in my wardrobe that Nikki wants to wear! I don't even bicker. Suddenly, the old familiar feeling surges in me; the old sigh comes out of my lips: *haaahh,* the long sigh of fear. We might as well enjoy the fun now, for there's a price to pay, I'm sure.

Later. *So when are you telling me the whole story, Dad? What happened that night, when you were out undercover, and you were shot? How come the backup didn't get there in time? Mom never told me the circumstances.*

Don't dredge that up, he says. *You've learned enough for now. Enjoy the magic of being protected. And leave the moon glass at home,* he orders sternly, as I'm about to slip it into my backpack. *It shouldn't be dragged to class, or to soccer practice. If you need empowerment, remember the rules: Like to like. As you own the magic in yourself, you will be able to bring out magic in others. And Link to link. You submit to higher magical authority.*

All right. I'll leave the moon glass in the room least likely to be rifled by Mom spying on me— the kitchen. *But could we put a little magic power in Josh?*

No, Josh is not magical, so you might as well put him out of your mind. People like you are portals, Lily—their magic is passed on from protectors like me. And we both have animal spirits. So forget about Josh. And leave the moon glass at home, or it will wreak havoc at school. Leave it here, or I'll strip it of its powers.

But I so wanted to wreak havoc at school!

19

There's no more satisfying feeling than being able to walk into school and not give a damn about the way you look. This must be how those Barbie girls walk around. Like they own the place. No wonder!

Nikki prances by Tony Meserve's locker—wearing my best sweatpants *and* my sexy yellow tank, I might add. Tony's there, and he's about to say something to Nikki, but then he takes another look at her, and his eyeballs bulge out. Then he watches her dance off to homeroom. I push the door to my locker, and as it shuts, it uncovers Andra.

"Hey," she says.

And I cut her off. "I'm not talking to you, I'll be late for Spanish."

"Don't try to put on this spooked act—I know you're not afraid of me. Hey, your team beat us fair and square." She grins—does she really mean that, or does she *know* that my dad helped, so she's *really ahead*? "I'm throwing a party at my place Saturday night—I'm inviting my team, your team, everyone. Come to my party, Lily."

"No, thanks. I don't want to."

"Why not? You won the game. You'll be the star."

Then she peers at my legs. I'm wearing jeans, so the scar from her cleats is not visible, but if I wore a bandage, its thickness would show. When she looks up, that inquiring feverishness is back in her eyes, that guessing which at first glance seems cheerful, but it's really hard and unreadable. That thin smile returns to her lips. "So you're coming?"

"No."

"Even your best friends will come. You want to be the one who stayed away? People don't stay away from my parties. I gave Holden a shopping list a mile long."

"Really. Good old Holden. How is he?"

"Normal enough to send on errands." Smiling

at her own joke, her lips gain a little pinkness, more personal, more animal-like at the same time, and I have zero doubt now: she knows *a lot*.

But I know too. I'm also fine with fear—fear's the rush before the battle. So be it!

I get very close to her, till we breathe in each other's faces; then she steps back—obviously if I stand my ground, she'll give way. "So be it!" I say. "Now get out of my way." I remember Nikki's phrase—thanks, Nikki. "I'm nexting you, Andra, you got it?"

She throws her hair back, walks off. Dressed like an ace, as usual, but her shoulders are stooped a little. Defied, defeated on the field, taken up on her challenge—it's taking a toll. I think cheerfully, Oh, Andra, I'm almost worried for you.

So, I had a glowing day.

But that glow dims when I come home, go into the kitchen the back way (noticing that the door is open—did I leave it unlocked?), and find a note from Mom:

Back at 7 P.M.—
how about we do something together?
Wait for me.

Mom doesn't have to sign her notes—I know the slanting strokes of her handwriting, and get tense every time I see them.

All right. Let's handle this new challenge.

I immediately go check the place where I hid the moon glass, on a top shelf in the kitchen, behind long-unused cookbooks. Mom stopped cooking; I haven't started yet. Tim cooks, not bad, but I hate his food—long live Grazia's pizza! I pry the books aside, squeeze my hand into the back space, can't find the little mirror.

I bring a chair, stand on it, tall enough now to pull the books out and examine the empty shelf.

The moon glass is not there.

Someone took it!

For an instant I just stand still, my brain going, who knew it was there? Only me. Did I plan to hide it here, but never did? Did I take it away and hide it someplace else? Then I notice traces of fingers printed on the thin dust gathered behind the books. Someone's hand reached in, just like mine now, felt around, pulled the moon glass out.

Mom. It had to be. She's a cop. A scavenger by nature.

Cops with kids know that their own houses might contain stashes of drugs, while their kids are smart enough not to hide a stash in their rooms, kids' rooms still get searched first. Kids also hide stashes in garages and sheds. In the house, they try to conceal them in plain sight, on shelves with knickknacks, or behind framed photos. I thought the spot I chose was safe. But Mom's been prowling. And she's already threatened to send me to that anger reduction school! Still, I keep searching.

Finally, I race into the alley behind the house, to look inside steaming trash cans. I poke through the trash. Nothing that even resembles Dad's little mirror. I rush back, wash my hands. Then I raid Mom's bedroom. She raided mine, I'm sure. Nothing. I try to raise Dad, no answer—he's at work, patrolling Heaven's ghettos.

My God. What shall I do?

I know that Nikki's out with her aunt. I know that Arielle's at home, but I'm not in the mood to call Arielle and get airhead advice. So that leaves Grazia.

I call her and find her at the pizzeria, where she sits behind the cash register when business is slow. When it's busy, her mom does. Now the place is practically empty, she tells me. No one's eavesdropping.

"Sit tight," Grazia says. "Don't tell your mom anything—wait till she brings it up. If she doesn't even mention it, someone else took it."

"Don't be ridiculous. Only my mom could've found it where I put it."

"Then wait till she asks you about it. You'll know what to do."

"All right, Grazia. I'll try."

I click off.

I slow down. I shower. I wait.

At a few minutes past 7 P.M. Mom is dropped off by Tim. She comes into the house, in uniform. I'm on the couch in the den, deep in my English Lit. She says hello, goes up and showers, comes back in jeans and a blouse, and pulls no punches. She raises her hand with the moon glass in it.

It's worth a try to act outraged. "How did you get that? You went through my stuff?"

"Not really," she says. "I wanted to pull out those cookbooks—I thought maybe if I started to make some meals again, we would feel more like a family. But I found this thing where I would've never put it, so I know you put it there." She pauses. I clench my teeth and remain quiet. She speaks again. "Padgett called me. She told me how far that thing with Andra went—and that you've been cutting classes. You want to tell me why?"

"I've cut a few classes here and there. My grades are still As and Bs. And that's because I pay attention in class, while other kids don't! Anyway, I don't know what Padgett's talking about."

She holds up the moon glass. "What about this?"

"It was Dad's. It was with his things in the garage."

"I know whose it was, but why do you have it?"

"I wanted something of his."

"Some kids carry little mirrors to cut cocaine on them—their little portable coke dish."

"Have you lost your mind?"

"Don't talk to me like that! You're really something, Lily. Slipping that story into the school paper would've never occurred to me." She actually smiles now, and I smile too—she gave me a compliment. "You have some nerve, Lily. You're not your mother's daughter for nothing."

My father's too, I smirk silently.

"Lily, I know . . . after you lost Dad, maybe you went through a period of denial, trying not to think of him, but now you're rediscovering him." I get so turned off when Mom starts speaking like a police therapist. "Then you started a cycle of rebellion—that too was to be expected." I'm getting so angry. But I remember Dad saying to me: *She's not magical, your mom.* Damn right! She's flat as a paddle, and I'm being nice! Denial, rebellion—that doesn't even begin to describe what's happening to me. But suddenly, I have this ugly feeling—Mom and I are so far apart. Is this how it felt between Dad and her?

"You can talk to me, Lily. You can tell me anything."

What a joke. But since I have to reply somehow, I reach out my hand. She hesitates, then puts the moon glass back in my hand. She's quiet, I'm quiet, but finally I ask, because I'm curious, "All right, why would you go nuts over a little thing like this?"

"I was looking for other little things. I'm lucky that's all I found."

I bristle again, ready to battle. "Like what?"

"Like bras or underpants you can't afford—girls your age are into shoplifting. Like a lot of boxes of breath mints—you pop three at a time, and you don't smell of alcohol. Shall I go on?" She checks my expression with that polygraph glance of hers. "Lily . . . did your father ever tell you something unusual about this mirror?"

"I don't remember. He told me stories when I was little. I liked them. . . ."

"I wish he hadn't told you those stories."

She says it harsh, but starts blinking quickly, and I get very tense—of all the people you hate to see cry, the worst is your mom. But then she breathes deeply—she's in control, it's over.

She says, "I'd like to have something of his too."

And then—I'm stunned—I reach to put the little mirror back in her hand. That's how much I'd like to help her. But as I touch it down onto her palm, she seems so scared. Of all people, I remember Andra just now—Andra made me feel that she knew something about me that I myself didn't know. Mom too makes me feels that *she knows*—yet she pushes the mirror back into my hand, and closes my fingers over it, because she wants to protect me, but the only way she knows how is to be silent.

"Stop cutting classes," she says at last.

"I'll stop," I reply. I put the moon glass on the kitchen table.

"Come on," she says. "I want to show you what

it's like on the street, in the parts of town you never go to."

"Mom, please!" I've been on such sociological trips before. "I know it's gruesome out there. You don't have to stick hell in my face to instill responsibility."

"That's not what I want to do," she says, with that contained sadness she'd learned to handle so well. Again, I want to be like her—100 percent like my mom the responsible single parent, the brave widow, the cop. But I can't—I'm not her. To be strong in my own way, it's the best I can wish for.

"Come on. My car's brake pads squeak so bad, we'll take Tim's Chevy."

And though I hate driving in Tim's Chevy, as if a younger me took over, I mouth obediently, "All right."

20

Driving in the Chevy. It feels so much like Tim. If mom's "flat," Tim must be worse than horizontal. He's a gulch dipping below the sea level—ditto his Chevy!

Anyway, I have no choice but to ride with Mom and listen to her.

"This is my beat," Mom says, plunging the Chevy into that murky inner harbor, the boarded-up part of downtown. "Whole streets of trash."

We roll past an old homeless woman covered in soot and filth from head to toe.

"Watch the traffic, Edna," Mom mutters at her. Edna doesn't hear. She lost something on the ground, so she's hunkering in almost zero light, patting the dirt, to find it.

We roll on. Then, crunched in the recessed space of a doorway, a man with his face and beard loaded with dirt holds up a needle—with one quick stab, he jams it into his neck.

"Mom," I shrill, covering my eyes.

"The junkies aren't really the problem," Mom says matter-of-factly. "They don't rob or kill very often—the gangs give them a fix now and then, to keep the place quiet. It's the gangs, of course . . ."

At the end of an alley, young girls and men of uncertain ages throw dice against a wall. The men are shirtless. The girls drink from big bottles of beer. I notice one of the girls—she could be my age. She's lowering a bottle, giving out a crazy laugh. . . . She could be me. . . .

"Yeah . . . ," my mother says, as if continuing an earlier thought. "They found one bleeding heart in the department, your dad, to go undercover here, to dress in dirt and sleep in dirt, for only a few weeks, Chief Noonan said, because there was a rumor that some super-gang was about to roll in. So Dad was to find out who the invaders were."

I'm frozen in my seat.

Mom scans the dead streets with live scavengers in them. No room for vulnerability.

"I told him, 'Turn down that assignment. We have a child.' He said, 'I can help those people. Everyone gave up on them, they even gave up on themselves—but as long as they breathe, they have some spark left. Someone has to get to it.'" Mom's voice starts shaking. " 'So how would you do that?' I asked him, though I already knew what he would try to do."

Now I know too.

He brought his magical animal spirits with him, to try to clean up this filth.

I gush suddenly, "Did he disobey the chief's orders?"

"He did. He saved a fellow cop, one that did the plunge here before him and was sucked in. Noonan had said to forget about him—that cop had become a druggie with a hundred tracks on each arm. Your dad got him out of here. He's alive—he's in San Diego someplace."

I'm breathless. San Diego . . . ?

The tat guy?

"Anyway, Dad's orders were to find out what super-gang was planning to take this hell over, then bring in an undercover unit, which Dad was training at the time, and when the new landlords came in, we would smash them before they could take possession. That was Chief Noonan's strategy, and he sold the department on it. But your dad told him, 'We must get the people on those streets in a program; we do that first, then we battle the gangs.' Your dad felt he needed time. He was also taking care of that cop who worked here before him—he got him in a rehab. Then the gangs sensed that the department wasn't behind your dad—they're good at that, believe me, and they hated your dad as much as some cops hated him, because wherever he went he broke all the crooked deals—so they leaked that Dad had brought in a gang of his own."

I freeze again. "What?"

"Uh-oh, what have we got here?"

I feel that I'm hearing her talking to my dad, when I was seven. The little Weregirls and I ate pizza around our messy kitchen table, and Mom rang Dad to check on how we were doing.

Easy night? Yep. No messy customers yet? No. Wait. Uh-oh . . .

Two men are shoving each other by a loading dock. One tackles the other, drops him with rapid fists to the face. The one on the ground pulls a knife, slashes . . . Blood flies. Mom grabs her cell, calls the po switchboard. Precise and quick.

"I don't have my piece with me, so I have to call this in," she explains, then guns the car into another alley. "See those girls?" She points to two girls walking a dog. I would've not even spotted them—they blend well—yet as we roll closer, I see that they're wearing flashy miniskirts, high heels, and fishnet stockings. One of them pulls the dog's leash, making the animal snarl at the passing car.

"The dog's their cover. They walk it around the block over and over, waiting for cars to pick them up. One girl goes with the trick; the other stays with the dog. If cops stop them, they say they were walking their dog." She grabs the cell again, makes another quick, precise report. "This one will go nowhere," she confides to me, refolding the cell.

"What do you mean?"

"Small stuff. No blood spilled, no action."

I know what she's thinking: Thank God that I'm not one of the girls with the dog. Or one of those girls being patted by filthy bums. Those, she'll bust sooner or later. Me, I'm the real reason why she is a cop.

I get it all. It sinks in real deep.

I clear my voice. "You were talking about Dad."

"Yeah. While rumors began that your dad had gone crooked, that he had his own gang down here, Noonan ordered Dad's own undercover team to raid the area, dressed in gang-banger outfits. Pretending to be the gang that was taking over. The rest of the department were ordered to go in as backup. I was backup. That's the spot," she says, and she points to the end of the block.

She stops the car.

"There was no wall back then," she says, her voice shaking.

I look. A few hundred yards ahead, the wasteland stops abruptly, shored up by a brand-new wall, with an iron gate. The gate is brand-new too; it's closed. A construction crane looms above the wall, motionless, like a frozen dinosaur. Heaps of sand and cement fill the space before the wall. Soft shapes of trees sway around that crane, inside the wall—like in a luscious private garden.

"Your dad took a bullet just beyond that wall, where that crane is now. After he was taken to the hospital and pronounced DOA, the bullet was pulled out of him and matched to the guns in the department, just in case he'd been shot by another cop. It didn't match anyone's gun. I was a rookie patrolwoman then—I was in the last detail of backup hurrying to the scene. When I arrived and jumped out of the car, they were picking up his body. . . ."

I think she'll cry. But then she doesn't. I don't either.

"Who owns that place now?" I ask, just to say something. I point matter-of-factly toward what lies beyond that wall and gate, and then I guess a split second before Mom replies: "That mover and shaker, Howard Hewlit. He bought it right before he moved his family back to Pasadena. I know because the city got awash in requests for building permits, all at the same time."

"He's building a new house?"

"There is a house there already. I think maybe he's adding to it."

I try to seem totally indifferent, though what I feel is, oh God, Andra and her family again, they're putting their stamp on everything. I look away from the brand-new gate. There is a small trailer parked among those heaps of cement, with a construction company's name painted on its side. It looks humble, dwarfed by the wall and the gate.

I look back at Mom.

She's back in time, still remembering.

"And then there was a sad new life, without a father for you, and rumors: the gang that was moving in were conjurers, tribal Indians, shamans. Because Dad was Indian. And Dad was under their spell. They had bizarre animals. They were there, lurking in the night, when the department raided the place. They could've been arrested, but they did some conjuring on the spot, and escaped. Your dad stayed on to cover for them—that's why he fell to that bullet, otherwise he would've vanished too. But the rumors died down fairly quickly. People don't keep talking about fallen cops."

I clear my throat. "That's it? You never found out more, never found out what really happened?"

"It wouldn't have brought him back. And I had to raise you and support the both of us the only way I knew how."

Then my memory flashes: I'm at the funeral again. . . .

That stranger who danced that strange dance, twirling in a circle . . .

He has Dad's features. . . .

He is from Dad's "gang."

Mom says, "I saw what they did to Johnny Parker. They ran him right out of town."

"Johnny Parker?"

"The guy your Dad helped. He came out of re-hab and started protesting that there were no conjurers, that Dad had been set up. They threw him out of the department—I doubt that he even received his pension. Later he moved to San Diego. I didn't try to find him, to ask him what he knew. I was so scared for both of us, I tried to prove I was a trustworthy cop. While all the time wondering, had I been more like him, if I could have helped him better."

She doesn't say it, but I hear it: *And he might have been alive. . . .*

"Mom . . ." I'm terrified of what she's been thinking for the last five years. "It wasn't your fault."

"I hope not. I loved your dad. More than I'll ever love Tim."

But with that, the feeling between us is broken again. Tim. There was no place for him here. She shouldn't have said his name. And yet she did.

There's still bitterness in her expression, like Dad left her with a mess on her hands. And she's still angry.

She doesn't say much after that. We drive back. When we get home, I open the car door to get out, but then I sit back inside. I want to say something sweet and helpful, like a real daughter. "Mom, I didn't know how hard it was for you. You saved my life."

Mom's back in the cop mode, I can tell by her tight face. "I saved you from the streets I just showed you, yes. The rest, you'll have to do yourself."

She puts her arms around me, clumsy and stilted—I feel her stiltedness, not her warmth. I don't know how to help her, and that breaks my heart. *I saved you from the streets I just showed you.* I can't be mad at her anymore. But I'm so used to being mad at her, it will be hard.

She tells me I can order a pizza for dinner.

I wonder how it ever worked out between my mom and dad. I seem to have been their only link.

I sit down on the couch while Mom looks inside the fridge and inside the pantry and declares that she might as well go out and do some shopping for a change. She makes herself a little list of essentials we sorely lack, then goes out to the store—and right away my dad speaks, volunteering his own side of the events: *As much as I don't want to admit it, if I had survived the shootout, your mom and me might not have stayed together.*

He never said anything like that before.

All these years, I thought my parents loved each other, but really it was a sham, a sham full of such good intent! They got married, she got pregnant with me, what could they do but stick it out?

Oh God. I'm so naive.

Our marriage wasn't a sham, he says. *We really did love each other. I fell in love with her the minute I saw her. I'm still in love with her. She has such great spirit.*

Had, I correct him. *She's so tired and bitter.*

Dad doesn't like hearing that, I can tell—he cuts me off. *Sometimes, differences are just too deep. That's why I'm warning you about Josh. There will be things about you that he will never understand. Things you will want him to be a part of, and he won't be—he doesn't have what it takes. That's why it's best to end it now, before it builds into anything. With all you're going through, do you really want to add a complicated relationship?*

Maybe my dad is right.

Of course I'm right.

If you're always right, why did you get shot? Why did you die?

I was right then too. It was what the situation called for.

But what happened? And who's Johnny Parker?

It's in the past, Lily. Nothing like that is going to happen again, so I don't see the point in going into it. Just know that I kept a good cop from going crazy, and perhaps being killed too.

Yeah, I say bitterly, *at the expense of all three of us.*

Everything happens for a reason, Lily . . . even when something sad or tragic happens. Don't judge before the real reasons of things are revealed.

But everyone judges, Dad. Look how quickly you passed judgment on Josh.

I'm looking out for you, and *for him. I don't want you to be hurt, or suffer the same heartache as your mom. Now I have to go.*

I know. As always, he has to go, Mom has to go. . . .

That's what happens when you're not a child anymore, and you don't want to be a child anymore, do you, Lily? You crave being a young woman.

He's right, I do. I'm all grown up. How convenient for him.

So, because I grew up, I'm alone now?

I look around; then I close my eyes. I open them again. And this is what I feel: yes, I'm alone.

I get up from the couch and pace into the

kitchen. I decide to call Josh—maybe I can talk to him about all this. And maybe let him down easy too. I pick up the phone, dial his number, but then I hang up after the first ring.

I look at the kitchen table, and the moon glass is gone. It's not where Mom left it.

I look for the moon glass all over the kitchen. I can't find it anywhere.

Then I remember that I'd left the kitchen door unlocked earlier. Was it still unlocked, when Mom and I drove out? I didn't check.

How pathetic: the cop family who won't lock their doors. The cop family who will get robbed in their own home!

I call Nikki and blurt out to her, "The moon glass is gone!"

"That's an interesting salutation."

"Sorry, I don't have time to be polite. When I went out with my mom, the moon glass was on the table. When we came back, it was gone."

"Well, I know I didn't take it. Who else knew about it?"

I know immediately. "Holden. But that means that Andra knows about it too. She sent him over to my place, with that camera. . . ." I gasp. "Wait a second, the camera! Did they get the camera too?" I'd shoved the broken camera in our pantry, where we store cans of tuna fish, Campbell soups, our "good" plates, and empty bottles with resale value that we never resell.

I rush over to the pantry. I find the camera where I hid it, behind the soups.

Then I get *crazy* crazy. Where's my log book?

With the cell in my hand, I rush up to my bedroom. I hid the log in my underwear drawer. Why am I so freaked? Who could harm me if they had my log book? What kind of like to like am I terrified about now? I wrote up—what? maybe two pages of it? And used that stupid cipher, gibberish to anyone else. I don't know, it doesn't matter, I plunge into my bedroom, heave out the drawer . . .

It's right there, where I left it. Maybe I should make some notation of where I hide things, to be less confused? Then I hear Nikki scream into my cell. She heard me trampling around. "Slow down, freako, you'll break your neck!"

"All right, all right. Here, I'm sitting down. No one stole the log yet."

"The log?" She remembers. "Oh yes. You never write in it."

"No I don't, but I'm having a meltdown. Call everyone, Nikki, tell them to come here, now!"

Minutes later we're together, examining the situation.

Only two people could've taken the moon glass—Holden, who knows where I live, and Andra, who also knows where I live; she rang my doorbell the other day. But then we remember what happened to Holden when he tried to grab the moon glass from me. We're totally divided about how he reacted to his own transformation. Maybe he liked it! And maybe he's still walking around in his hairy version! The important issue is, would he have the guts to come near my house again, to steal the moon glass?

Nikki says, "Maybe Andra can make him do a lot of things. The question is, what are we going to do now?"

"But it's not proven that he stole the moon glass, or that Andra has it now," Arielle says.

I snap, "Arielle, you've been behaving really disloyal to me, really treacherous and devious. You did your hair blond, you constantly disagree with me—whose side are you on?"

"Yours, I mean ours—what the hell's with you?"

"What are you going to do, Lily?" Grazia asks quietly.

"I don't know. I'll keep trying to get through to my dad."

"You're not going to get to your dad anytime you want," Grazia says. "I think that tells you something: he wants to see how you'll handle certain things by yourself."

"That dawned on me too," I counter. "Speaking to me from Heaven doesn't mean he stopped being a parent. But thanks."

"It's easy," says Arielle. "Andra's party is Friday—that's in three days. We go to the party. If she has the moon glass, we take it back from her. What else is there to discuss?"

My pride, for one thing—after all that happened, how could I be a part of Andra's party?

But my friends are dying to go. A party in the mansion that Howard Hewlit just bought. "What a great place to show off," Arielle says dreamily. "The whole school's going to be there. Lily, you had lunch with Andra, she challenged you, you challenged her back, we had a match, we won— to go to her party is good sportsmanship."

"You sound just like Padgett. What about how she injured me?"

"But you're all healed up. Look." Arielle slaps my leg where the cleats cut into it, and I feel no pain whatsoever, so I can't even wince or anything.

"Come on," adds Nikki, astonishing me even further. "I'll be wearing a skirt for the first time in five years! This will be the year's biggest party. I bet even kids from L.A. will be coming."

I look at Grazia for help.

"It could be fun," Grazia chimes in.

"Yeah, why does everything have to be so serious?" Arielle asks. "If Andra stole the moon glass, let's confront her at the party."

So it's settled. They're going to Andra's party.

And I'm not.

Only three days until Friday.

21

Friday morning.

We went out with Nikki and got her a dress, and she declared, by way of trying to convince me to go, that she removed the hooks on all parts of her—maybe she'll meet someone at the party. I tried to snicker that if she does, she'll be ready.

All my friends are dying to go. Grazia hopes to hook up with this kid she likes, the hot nerd who writes poetry, Goldoni. Nikki's excited to show her skinny legs below the hem of a dress. Arielle is ready to meet the world.

I'm not going.

About once every half hour or so, I find a way

to say to my friends, "I haven't changed my mind. I'm not going!" Whether the conversation warrants it or not.

"I heard that Andra invited the Sagemont team, all of them," Arielle says.

"You stop that," I threaten, "or we'll stop being friends, Arielle, right here and now! I've already explained to you, my dad wants to see that I'm responsible, and this is the best way." I feel like I'm palpitating. "Not to go to the party of someone I hate (I *abhor* Andra, *irregardless*!), and win his trust and respect, all in one shot!"

"What if Josh decides to go to the party?"

"I know who would like him there more than anyone. Arielle, you want to know if Josh is going? Here!" I grab my cell and dial Josh.

He answers, out of the noise of some industrial site—then I remember that he's now working for his dad, who's a building contractor.

"Hey. You at work?"

"Yeah, my dad's finishing a driveway on someone's estate—actually, I think it belongs to that rich guy everyone's talking about, Andra's dad."

"Huh? I can't hear you!"

He says it again, slowly. "That rich guy, Howard

Hewlit? My dad's been hired to finish a delivery drive at the back of his property."

"I don't care. What are you doing tonight?" Before he can even answer: "You want to get together?"

A beat of surprise on his part. "Yeah," he answers.

"Want to go to the mall, and get a Coke?" I sound totally silly. "And maybe, we take in a movie?" I feel like there's a bubble with words in it coming out of my mouth, like in a cartoon.

"Uh . . . sure. My father has two cars. I'll ask to borrow the Cherokee, the one he doesn't usually take to work. Though it's got some cans of paint in the backseat—I hope you don't mind."

"Oh no, no. Being picked up in a utility vehicle loaded with industrial materials is just my style." I look aside at the girls: *I'm cool, and I got a date, huh?* For some reason, they're acting uptight. I can't read their moods. "So, eight o'clock?"

"Sure, I'll pick you up."

"Bye."

I fold my cell.

Then I say, as regal in my tone as I can possibly manage, "You see, Arielle? I got plans *overlapping,* exactly at that time!" Arielle shakes her head, which is even blonder than last time; she used that shampoo again. "And maybe, if Andra has some fabulous cake, you bring some back for Josh and me."

"Wait a second," says Arielle. "Seriously, Lily, I thought we were all going to Andra's party, to show off our new powers, right? I mean, she's got the moon glass, maybe, but we, we've got our animal spirits, right? Or else, what was the point of all that stuff that happened the other night?"

"Right," confirms Nikki. "There was ice flying in the air, and then your dad spoke to us, and we saw that magical light—is that like, not a thing anymore?"

I think, Jesus, what did my mad dad start?

How am I to tell them that I don't know, I don't know? You know? I got really so scared, totally terrified, after glimpsing the place where my dad was shot. I'm still pretending to be in control, but I haven't spoken to my higher protector, Dad, in several days, and it feels like someone's blocking him every second. And that person might be my own mother. And now that I think of it, could it be that while he and Mom were together, Mom lessened his magical powers, and as a result, he was less protected when Chief Noonan invaded the ghetto and got him gunned down?

I know it was Noonan. I have no doubt anymore.

But I have no proof. And just now, I don't even have the moon glass.

Not quite the best time to live up to my friends' expectations, and . . . look at them! Even Grazia, the best and most solid, whispers when I look at her, "I thought we were going to be really magical from now on, have magic in our life in everything, and I'm not talking fixing our grades. But like, love, for instance."

"Yeah," says Nikki, swaying on high heels in front of me. "I thought we were in for love spells and things. Where are my spells, Lily? Where's my personal power?"

"What about this?" I ask, pointing at her improved silhouette. "Not good enough? You want to make guys fall on all fours before you, so everyone can see? It's not like that."

"Then you don't know what it's really like either," says Nikki. "Come on, girls, let's go to the party without any particular powers. As ourselves!"

And that seals it. They're going, without powers. Never underestimate the draw of a good party!

Only now I realize I too wanted to go, to be part of it, even if it's her manse, her décor, her servants, caterers, valets, et cetera. Her glory. I'd still walk into it like the one who defeated her, the one and only person who stood up to her. I'd still be a tough act to follow—and that might impress Josh more than a glass of Coke at a Formica table in a food mall. I'm ready to give in, to say, "Girls, I want to go too!" Even if I go as poor old me. But some sort of pitiable sense of myself that I recognize as entirely familiar, the me I thought I'd changed forever, holds me back. Let them go to that glitzy gala. I'll go to the mall.

I slow down. I study.

I wash the dishes.

Every time I do something like that, I stop and throw my shoulders back and stand glumly as if Dad could take my picture from up there, for my certificate of humble endurance and anonymous maturity. You see this, Dad? Is this enough? Do I have to stoop even lower?

He's not talking to me.

And it drives me crazy.

All right, it was a dream. Totally.

So let's concentrate on going to the mall. I'll be wearing my best knockoffs, and a white shirt that I wash and press myself, and add light starch on the collar. Very plain and clean—me.

And black shoes—a pair of Capezio flats that I saved in very good condition by practically living in my sneakers.

I ask the girls to drop in before they drive to the party. I want to see them.

They come, dressed to the nines. Nikki, in a real dress, has an almost elfin appearance, cute as everything.

I'm glumly happy for them.

They've been here one minute, and there's a knock at the door. I open the door and I see Josh on the porch. He's in jeans, and a work shirt, and loafers that make me burst out laughing: he has a trailer park/preppy kind of look.

I'm resplendent in my white shirt, so he clears his throat. "Hey!"

"Hey. You're so on time."

The girls were still in the house when he knocked. They troop out to see him, and Arielle quips right away, "So, you won't be pining alone, Lily. You'll be plenty busy." She chuckles. Then she leads the girls out, past Josh, toward her mom's Camaro, which she borrowed for the night.

"Catch up with us at the party," Nikki says.

"No chance," I whisper fiercely, though I still pace out after them—from that pure habit we have, to always trail after each other.

The girls drive off. I turn back and face Josh.

He shaved carefully; his lips have that slight milky look, just in between boyishness and man-hood. But his shoulders swell up his shirt; his muscles look ripe and round everywhere. I find him so attractive, I think maybe we'll hook up first, and after that, I'll tell him it can't work be-tween us.

"Ready to go?"

"Sure."

"If you change your mind, I'll take you to that party. All your friends are going."

"You be my friend this evening." Which re-minds me that I have to tell him, and it feels so hard. I think he really likes me.

"Let's go."

I start for his Cherokee. I glimpse cans of paint arranged in the backseat, with a piece of tarp par-tially covering them, and decide that I'll ignore them: this car will be our glamo limo for the next ten minutes. Because in ten minutes I'll tell him we're friends, but that all that happened last time I saw him, in my backyard, when he put his hands on my waist, is off. Easier to tell him before we get to the mall, while he's busy driving. Josh opens the door.

"How chivalrous," I comment.

"I'm old-fashioned," he says. "A man opens the door when he takes a lady out."

Great corny line, and how well it works. I'm a lady and he's a man, and old-fashioned.

And what about love? Can love be really strong, yet not strong enough to break through, from the magical to the nonmagical? The Beatles said all you need is love. Maybe Mom and Dad didn't love each other enough. Maybe Josh and I could be the supernatural realm's own Romeo and Juliet? I'm getting ahead of myself. I try to think of what to tell him. Tell him everything, I advise myself impetuously—maybe he won't want to start anything after he hears your whole story. Then I won't have to decide.

So I start talking, and we're still in traffic.

I fill him in about my mom and dad, and how it didn't work out because she's not magical. He gets the hint.

He acts offended—after driving very smoothly, he speeds up, then has to brake hard behind another car.

"Can't you ask your dad to make me magical?"

"I don't think it works that way," I reply—but I become excited. He looks angry, and cute, and more boyish than before. He plunges the Cherokee down the ramp into the mall's garage. The barrier blocks his way. He rips out the parking ticket, the barrier lifts, and he hurtles into the garage. "That sucks. It's not fair, and your dad doesn't even know me."

"I know he doesn't, but he knows you're flat." Whatever insult he hears in that statement, he gets even angrier; he finds a parking spot, pulls in jerkily while I'm having the greatest lousy time of my life, just looking at him and thinking, Let's see how far and through how much he's willing to go for me.

Then he controls himself and tries to laugh. "I'm not good enough for you, is that it? I'm from the wrong side of the tracks?"

"It's not like that. My dad's speaking from experience, because it was so hard between him and my mother, and they did love each other, *and they were married*!"

"But if they never got together, they would have never had you!" Pretty worked up again, he gets out and bangs the door on his side, but still opens my door, then takes my hand to help me out. "Do you ever think that maybe your dad is just making this up, so his daughter remains this baby girl, instead of growing up, going out with guys, whatever? Just because he communicates from beyond the grave doesn't mean he's ready to let go of you."

"So . . . are you fighting for me?" I flirt.

He's silent, as if pondering. Maybe he *is* fighting for me, while holding my arm to help me over some parking dividers.

I look up. Just ahead of us, I see a young kid dragging a dolly loaded with ice cream cartons, big ones; they look like five gallons each. He's got the logo of Coldstone Ice Cream embroidered on his shirt, and the cartons are stacked up in a pile taller than him. Behind him steps Holden, fussily directing. "Go on, that Jag over there, easy, *watch out!*" A big carton falls off the dolly, caves in on one side when it hits the concrete. "Careful!" Holden yells. Then he pops up the trunk of the Jag, which is parked two rows from Josh's Cherokee.

I start running toward them. When I plant myself right behind the Jag, the guy from Coldstone is unloading the ice cream into the trunk, which seems too small for that load. "We've got to put some in the backseat," he says.

"It'll stain the seat," Holden snaps.

"Hey Holden," I say, "Andra forgot to buy ice cream?"

He spins around, as if the sound of my voice stung him.

When he sees me, he looks like he might jump behind the wheel and peel off with the ice cream still only half loaded—then he notices Josh, and freaks even more. "Get them in there!" he yells at the Coldstone kid. As he rushes to the driver's door, fumbling for his keys, he mumbles, "I didn't forget, but we ran out already—the party started at three." He coughs from nervousness, glances shiftily at me. "You coming?"

"Can't you tell I'm not?"

"Good!" The ice cream kid is finished. He lingers, wiping the sweat off his face, waiting for a tip—but Holden slams the trunk and back door shut, jumps behind the wheel, and revs up so hard we're almost blown back by the fumes from the shiny twin exhausts. Holden backs up hard, right toward us, as if wanting to run us over. We jump aside.

I don't know when I started to run back toward the Cherokee. I find myself tearing at the passenger door. "Open it up, Josh!"

Josh rushes to unlock, gasping, "He's gone already, even if I try, I got zero pickup compared to him!"

"I don't care, follow him!" I throw myself in the passenger seat.

"Lily, what are you . . . ?"

"Follow that Jag!"

"You nuts?" But he's behind the wheel already; he cranks up the Cherokee; in a second, we're speeding to catch Holden.

He's way ahead; I can barely see his taillights.

"I'll lose him," Josh says, and I think, *Weregirl, help me!* Just then, the Jag stops way ahead at the exit gate, blocked by the lowered barrier. Josh careens across some empty parking slots, gets right behind him. Holden's unclear silhouette seems to throb in his seat: he's fumbling for his parking ticket.

And that's it—he can't find his ticket!

I start laughing with fits.

Holden revs up and splinters away, through the barrier as if it were a matchstick.

Josh gapes, but then guns through right after

him. We hurtle up the ramp. I can hear two sets of tires screeching madly. I'm thrown against Josh, I fish for the seat belt, pull it over my chest and click it in, and gasp an explanation. "Holden stole the moon glass!"

"Whaaa . . ."

"Just don't lose him. I'll explain more later!"

Outside in the street, we catch up with the Jag. I can't even see Holden, hidden by the pile of ice cream cartons—but I'm sure he's gawking in his side mirror to check if he's followed. He slips the Jag in and out of lanes like an eel, so Josh has no choice but to honk and maltreat the traffic around the Cherokee, braking hard and close behind back bumpers, darting ahead again. . . . I begin to laugh: he's ready to do this for me, and I don't have to tell him *tonight* that we're not good together. At least not till this chase is over. I get so focused on not losing the Jag, I don't even know where we are. The Jag with the Cherokee in tow burns a red light, and we're suddenly on those scummy streets. Like in a time warp of the other night, I see those girls walking their dog—suddenly, Josh brakes so hard, he has to slap his hand onto my shoulder—even with the belt on, I almost fly into the windshield.

The Jag is stopped right in front of that brand-new wall that Mom showed me the other night.

I look away from it. About thirty yards away, among those heaps of cement, I see that little trailer again. "Does your dad work out of that trailer?" I ask, remembering what Josh told me at Tapas: his dad was building something in Pasadena, in an area that used to be a slum.

"Yeah," he replies. "He uses it as his office. He built that driveway, redid the wall, and put in the gate last week."

"But that's where Andra lives!"

"So?" he asks innocently.

Meanwhile, the Jag's headlights blaze onto the brand-new gate like they'll start burning holes in it.

Holden activated some remote control. The gate begins to lift, he guns in, and I shriek at Josh, "Go! Go!" But a Cherokee isn't a Jaguar. Josh finally moves forward but then brakes: the gate's already dropping back in place.

"Why'd you stop?"

"You crazy? I'd need a tank to ram through that!"

Meanwhile, Holden and his Jag are inside. I

bump the Cherokee's door open, jump out—in time to hear, from behind the wall, a big screech of tires and that inimitable boom of a car hitting some hard obstacle.

"Where are you going?" yells Josh.

I don't reply. I run forward.

22

The wall stands about eight feet high. It's made of aged-looking masonry, perhaps to match some French mansion inside. The big trees beyond, gum trees and pines, hang their branches over the bricked-up top of the wall. I'm pumped like before scoring a goal, yet a sharp chill runs down my neck.

Josh grabs my elbow. "What are you doing?"

"Getting ready to climb over this wall. You can wait for me here if you want."

"Do you even know what you're getting yourself into? What's on the other side?"

"That scum's estate, and trust me, I can handle

her!" *Maybe tonight I'll get all the answers I wanted. Don't even think about stopping me, Dad!*

I put one foot on the protrusion of a lower brick. Josh realizes I mean it. He drops a knee to the ground, then latches his fingers, making his hands into a stepping platform. I step on his hands; he lifts me up; I grab the top of the wall. I'll scratch my hands pretty bad, but I don't care. Up, and over!

When I'm up on top, I see a driveway, and the Jag, stopped only a few yards up, its nose in a gum tree's trunk. Holden lost control and crashed off the driveway, into the tree. He's out of the Jag and rolling around on the driveways' concrete, which is muddied with ice cream—he smashed the car hard enough to pop the doors and the trunk open, and the ice cream is flowing!

Just then, huffing hard, Josh propels himself onto the wall somehow and bumps me. He's so muscular and heavy, we bail together onto the other side. All around that new driveway, the grounds are very unkempt. There's piles of old leaves, so it doesn't hurt too bad when I land—but I'm up again in a blink. Josh gets up wincing, but then he lunges ahead, bum-rushes Holden into more ice cream cartons, which keep falling from the car's backseat. Holden punches Josh, but Josh smashes him right in the nose, and into those cartons, popping lids, springing geysers of vanilla and chocolate! Josh pulls himself from that mess, pins slippery Holden in a double arm bar.

"Frisk him," he says. "Maybe he got that thing."

My hands are scratched from the wall—I feel it when I pat Holden on all his ice-cream soaked sides, icy and wet. I pull stuff from his pockets. Another set of keys, a soaked pack of cigarettes, a cell clammy with rocky road. He doesn't have the moon glass.

"Get out of here," slurs Holden. "Get out of here, or you're in for it! Andra's got the moon glass. What do you got, Lily?"

I've got myself, I think fiercely.

Josh shakes Holden. "Where's the house?"

Despite all this chaos, we can hear voices, and music. Not far. Ahead, there is a rambling construction site, with low scaffoldings. Now I see that it's attached to an old house, but the house is just an old Pasadena craftsman house, larger than the one I grew up in, but no mansion. It's being enlarged and remodeled.

I shout at Holden, "Where's the party, creep?"

Holden laughs.

And suddenly, he vanishes! Like he was never there.

"What the . . . ," Josh stammers. "Where'd he go?"

We breathe wildly, and listen—there is rock music coming from beyond that construction area. By the construction, the ground's all turned up and muddied. Peering past the construction, I see a faint glowing ahead.

"Where did that idiot go?" Josh keeps mumbling. Then, overwhelmed by the disappearance, and the strangeness of the place, he asks, "Are you sure we should be here?"

"No," I gasp, "I'm not sure of anything! Go back if you want!" Maybe if Josh goes back, Dad will signal to me again. *Dad, will you please give me some instructions?*

Nothing!

But Josh takes my arm. He tries to speak without stammering—he's scared, I can tell. "Do you think they're missing their ice cream?" he jokes, pointing back to the mess of leaking cartons. Then he gently prods me along. "All right, now we're here, let's find out what this is. . . ."

Then, a cloud must have moved, because the

moon kindles up above us, sickle shaped, over the unfinished construction, and the unkempt garden around it. We advance. I can hear my own breath.

We pass an old oak; the knotted branches bulge in the dark as if coming alive. The bark shimmers, reflecting the moonlight. The knots start glowing like black feral eyes. They open and close, as if in winks. Josh takes a deep breath, but keeps bumping me ahead. "Hey, you helping me or hiding behind me?" I ask.

He huffs, "Both!" Even as freaked as we are, we still laugh.

I keep looking around, still waiting for Holden to reappear. Weeds and rotting plants run over the roots of trees, like lunatics with storming hair. Mad and raving, arms outstretched, as if trying to warn us. Then again, like a tease, I hear voices. Party noises. The reassuring echoes of today. We can't be too far from the house.

Chills run through me. Footsteps are crushing the dried-up grass. Approaching.

"Get down," I whisper, and pull Josh down, and we hunker motionless in the grass.

Nothing.

We step forward again. Then . . .

Some kind of animal is coming toward us, its

nails clicking on newly laid concrete. A small, benign-looking dog, like a poodle; he moves through the moonlight. Then he sees us, runs like a gunshot, inside that still-unfinished structure.

I suddenly know—there are answers in there.

"I'm going in," I say.

Josh nods, and follows. We start hustling down a shallow set of steps.

Darkness.

Then, the darkness thins out. We're in some underground room. Dumped luggage, many pieces, most of them open and empty. For some reason, I think that they've been purchased all over the world. We pick our way through the clutter, past old furniture, caved-in couches, a big mirror with spots, drippy like from dried splattered blood. And the space ahead seems to stretch, to elongate suddenly, as if to reinforce what this is: a limbo of loss, carelessness, and lack of hope? Who the hell lived here before? Whose property did Howard Hewlit take over? Something breathes in the shadows.

That dog's in front of me. He's looking at me. Cocks his head, studies me. I'm frozen. He sniffs. In his eyes, there's something so twisted and sad—an emptiness beyond description. I shiver, and the dog burrows in a large puddle of books scattered on the floor.

Josh pulls on my wrist. "Let's get the hell out of here."

"No. I have to find out what this place is."

"Even if it's dangerous?"

I don't have time to answer—I glimpse a standing rack filled with big books. Leather-bound. In a blink I'm before them: old tomes, weather-torn.

Josh touches a book. It falls down before him, as if in slow motion, and the cover pops up. That dog's face springs from the pages.

I can't even scream. The other books come alive, fuse into a whirlwind, a swirling cloud of nightmares. We turn fast, but our retreat's blocked by another whirlwind.

Get away, Lily, get ah . . . way. . . . My father's voice is fuzzy like bad reception.

But where could I get away? Josh throws his arms around me. The whirlwinds press near, an inch from drowning us—but then the tattoo on Josh's arm blinks alive! As if an inner light breaks out of the weregirls carved on his skin! I'm so scared, I scream like in an old horror movie, but perhaps I add power to the tattoo—its light seems to blow back that gusting evil. The whirlwind sucks back into the books, and the books slam shut.

I can feel Josh's heart pumping, because he's squeezing me tight—and now my dad comes through almost clearly.

Turn back, Lily. You've gone far enough.

I don't want to turn back. I want to know all about you. And what the hell was that animal?

You know enough. The Breed is still asleep. Maybe they won't wake up.

What the hell is the breed?

The Breed, he repeats, and the old books of magic suddenly blow away, revealing the floor, which shines dimly; and right under its surface I see beastly shapes, many, frightening because their contours are unclear, as if shaped by a dream in progress, but . . . they are in front of me. I don't have the time to pinch myself now—they are right under that glassy surface, stirring gently, as if hibernating.

Lily, don't go farther. You know you're protected and that's enough. If you go on ahead, you'll give evil what it wants.

I'll give evil what it wants? How can I do that?

They want an encounter. They want a face-off

with you! Turn back. And get Josh out of there; he can't handle it.

Maybe Josh is guessing that I'm having this unearthly dialogue; he's gawking at me. *He can protect himself!* I insist.

No, he can't. The tattoo saved him. Josh has no idea what to do.

I don't care. I want to know your world, and if you won't show it to me, I'll find out for myself!

Think of the rules, he says, and I can tell he's exasperated. *Like to like—and link to link! And you're making this hard, because that boy's jamming me, though he doesn't even know it!*

Well, tough, I'll rely on myself then!

I pull Josh by the hand. We make it to a doorway, with its hanging old door open. Through it and out . . .

Suddenly . . . we are by a large French mansion, which is reflected, all three stories of it, in an oversized swimming pool. The jarring, reassuring noise of a band, kids running around—a flood of what's real and normal, invading us, making fear drain away. Josh pulls on my hand, and when I turn around—he kisses me on the lips. Awkward, but warm—scent of wet skin, full lips, magic.

Then he steps back. Even against the pulsing lights of the party, he looks like he blushed.

Oh God, what a great quick peck. Now I want a real kiss.

But then out of the corner of my eye, framed in the house entrance, Andra stands in a dress that shines dark, like a heavy old wine. She steps out toward me.

"Glad you could make it, Lily. I thought you really chickened out. All your friends are here. Come."

I don't move. But Josh staggers closer, and looks from her to me, speechless.

"Come with me," Andra says.

She moves fast, grabbing me by the hand. The touch of her hand is strange: feverish, and scary. I look back for Josh, but Andra's so quick, she pulls me across a crowd—Josh is way behind us now. We step into an atrium so large, a whole graduation crowd could fit in it—I can tell there are kids here from all over the southland.

Josh is sucked back among hundreds of girls and boys.

The party's in full swing. Strobe lights and music pumping. Andra weaves me inside. I let her pull me along. We step into a hangar-sized place;

turns out to be the mansion's kitchen. There are some waiters here, taking food on plates from several cooks, and diving back with it into the party.

I gasp. "Nikki!"

I can't believe this. Nikki sits on an island counter, surrounded by a circle of jocks. She sits with one leg dangling, and smiles, so sure of herself. Two guys arrive from opposite directions, each holding a tall drink, and one of them is Tony Meserve, who hurries to get here first, so he trips, and falls—almost on all fours! But he manages to salvage the drink, then presents Nikki with it.

I'm about to yell with laughter when Andra pulls my hand. We orbit into a large foyer where the DJ is set up. Arielle whirls around here, one with the music. She sees me, waves at me. The crowd hops, Arielle hops faster than all the others, and when I yell at her, "Where's Grazia?" she laughs and points toward a door at the other end of the foyer.

She smiles in that way that girls understand instantly: Grazia's in there, and she's receiving some sweet attention.

"Here," Andra says to me, like a caring hostess.

And she leads me into that door: a library, where a bunch of kids sit on the floor—Grazia sits next to that hot nerd who writes poetry, Goldoni. He's setting down a bottle, ready to spin it. Well, if he's such a genius, I hope he gets to kiss Grazia at the first try! Grazia doesn't even see me. She leans over, whispers something to Goldoni. . . .

It's like I'm in some altered dimension where all my friends act totally happy. I should feel happy too. . . .

Andra motions me to a staircase. It's packed with a million kids sitting on the steps, boys and girls, talking, sipping drinks. Andra cuts right through them, up. We step on a landing. I look down—Arielle is dancing right below, in a crowd that takes their cues from her. She's leading, moving so uninhibitedly that everyone twirls and twirls with her. Arielle's so focused and secure with herself; she's no longer a teenager, she's a woman.

"What did you do to my friends?" I ask, shivering, pulling my hand away, but Andra doesn't let go. She totes me along like I'm her Fendi bag, toward the end of that landing. A door is open there.

"What did *you* do to your friends," she counters, "and what did you do to me?"

What's she talking about?

Dad, where are you? What's going on? I plead

silently, and he comes in very broken.

I'm watching the Breed. . . . Someone has to. . . .

Andra leans her face close to mine and smiles. Her dress is the color of wine, and the color alone is going to my head.

"You want to see my room, Weregirl?" she asks, and steps on, not even looking back to see if I follow her.

I tell myself: Maybe she's hiding the moon glass in her room. . . . This is my chance to get it back. . . .

And so we step . . . into Andra's room.

23

A ndra's room is huge, a penthouse in itself.
I lose most of my brain skills, just from
the size of this girl's bedroom. All I can do just
now is register with my eyes.

The dreamiest furniture, and a massive four-
poster . . .

A totally sick TV: a huge plasma flat screen
hanging on the wall opposite her bed . . .

She even has a kind of kitchenette to one side,
with a big fridge that looks like a shiny aluminum
capsule—the kind scientists bury in the ground,
for other millennia to find out about us? Well,
they'll sure find out about Andra! The kitchenette's got a stove, counters, the fridge, even an

elaborate espresso maker—following my glance, Andra smiles. "This is where I make myself breakfast in the morning."

I nod. "Very practical. Why call the house helicopter, to shuttle you to the actual breakfast room?"

She grins. "You still got your big mouth. Want to check out my clothes?"

Oh yes! The clothes . . .

The clothes are scattered in racks and racks poking out of walk-in closets that line the space where the personal kitchen stops and the private dressing room starts. "I'm sorry, I don't have the patience," I mumble, and turn toward the bed, seeking some relief from opulence, something just slightly more normal, but . . . the bed is as merciless as everything else here. It's a square mile of a bed, with ten cubic yards of pillows and things . . . and . . . books.

There is a multiswitch by the bed, and Andra flicks the top button on. The lights go out *only above the bed*. Other lights, round and colored, start gliding around in the ceiling. Andra's got a planetarium built into the ceiling, with the moons and stars lit so realistically, they're breathtaking.

If I reach my hand up I can touch the pock-marked cheek of the moon.

And it all floats above Andra's bed.

"Yeah, my room's not bad," she agrees casually.

I look at the books spread on top of the rumpled bedsheets. Old books. Leather covers. One of them is open: I bend over it and see notes scribbled on the pages, as if in a hurried hand.

"That's what amateurs like me have to study, while naturals like you get it at birth," she says, and there is again that lone honest note in her tone: this is what she envies me for!

I step back because I'm afraid the books will open and waft out another whirlwind like in that basement, and I trip on the marble lip of a sunk-in fountain, set on the other side of the bed.

Good for a nice cool dip in the morning. I'm sorry I'm not sick to my stomach, so I can spew in Andra's fountain, but . . . I'm not! Wealth can be so breathtakingly pretty!

Andra motions me to sit next to her on the bed, by the fountain, and I do. I hear a faint call from Dad: *Walk away*. But it's like in another life.

"You're so lucky," Andra says.

Huh?

I mutter, "Why would you think I'm lucky? You're the one who's lucky. Look at all this. . . ."

"No, no, you're even luckier. Because," she says, with that resentful honesty, "you've had pain and loss in your life. Your father was killed, your mother's out there facing bullets, and that's exciting, that's special!"

"It's not exciting! It sucks!"

"Oh come on, Lily," she says, as if it's obvious, "pain and loss make a girl unusual. What's more exciting than tragedy? Beats clothes, guys, drugs . . . all that other stuff that I'm done with." Her eyes are checking on me feverishly. "You *know*?"

I *don't* know. To think that the loss I had to endure is exciting—that's really too confusing. I try to speak. I try to sound open. "Andra, it's not at all what you think. I cried so many nights."

"But then you were granted powers!"

Have I been? I wonder. Is that how loss rewarded me?

"You were chosen as a portal. And I'm lucky that I was ready when I was chosen as a portal too, but without you, it would have never happened, you know?" I hear it again, her envy, mollified by a kind of gratitude, and her gratitude too is more like wonderment about herself. I was a tool. I was really put in her path!

"Like to like!" she exclaims.

I nod. Like to like.

I'm so scared, I think fiercely, like to like, my friends, where are you? I need you!

"The Breed is choosing me as a portal," she says, as if she just won prom queen.

"Dad, you said the Breed was asleep," I whisper out loud, by mistake.

"You see." She smiles really happily. "How can you deny what you got?"

I'm speechless.

"The Breed is waking up, and they're going to choose me. I realized it when I took your moon glass. You want it back, Lily?"

"So you stole it?"

"It didn't help me at all; it turned into an ordinary mirror. But the fountain changed—look." Andra flicks on another switch, and the waters of the fountain swirl. I peer in; the monsters I glimpsed in the dark of the construction site are floating in the fountain water.

I see the Breed.

They float, as if in sleep, and they remind me of the weregirls, but . . . I glimpse their slit eyes.

They're demonic. Everything that's puppyish, joyful, lively in the weregirls is mutated here—these are the demonic weregirls. Matted fur, slit eyes, carbuncled flesh.

"Like to like," Andra says again. "So thanks, Weregirl, I knew you were the real thing, and I knew you'd make it happen for me."

"But they're asleep," I say, hoping against hope, pointing to the Breed sleeping with eyes half open, in drowned hibernation.

"They're waking up," she says. "I can feel it."

I reach over to that switch, shut off the fountain.

"Andra, you have no idea what you're talking about. This is not like reading spells in a book. This is the real thing, with real fear and pain, real death and darkness. You don't know what you're dealing with."

"Yes, I do," Andra says, "and I'm ready. I want it."

"There are other ways to be magical. I can talk to my dad; maybe you could be a weregirl."

Andra laughs. "The Breed is choosing me as their portal," she whispers excitedly, "but I'm choosing them too." Like Holden's face did on that roof, her face morphs so quickly, I can't tell what I saw. Subliminal, and terrifying. *Slit eyes, foes to man . . .*

The Breed's already in her.

As my heart does jumping jacks in my throat, Andra laughs and pulls out the moon glass.

"Join forces with me, Lily," she says, at once threatening and seductive. "And I'll help you avenge your dad."

I gasp. "Why avenge? What do you know about how he died?"

"Not much more than you, but we can find out more together."

It's hard to say what I feel—maybe a deep sense of desecration. The fear I felt in the basement dissolves within me. What I was trying to tell her, she told it to me: even if we are magical, we have a choice what side we choose. Seeing the moon glass in Andra's palm, I feel her desecrating touch so intimately; she's rubbing her manicured hand over my love for my dad, his magical stories, my childhood and growing up, my loss. I can't allow it. She won't tarnish what my dad and I share, even if I have to keep fighting her.

"Fine," I say. "We'll settle this right now." And then I laugh. My weapon is the moon glass, this little magical object—it's really tiny! While Andra, who wasn't granted the moon glass, was granted a grandiose view of evil in that fountain built right inside her vast, excessive, endless bedroom. How in character with who she is!

Deep within me, I ask my weregirl to come into my being, to fill me with the power of our spirits. If my summons will ignite Andra one hour earlier—like to like—so be it. I'm prepared. *Come to me, weregirl!*

Instantaneously, Andra shifts into a hideous beast . . . and yet she looks smart too, chic somehow. Hip evil!

I feel the muscles in my legs and arms ripple like the disturbed waters in that fountain. I charge, slam Andra to the floor, and again, out of the bedroom, into the hallway. Even in her hideousness, she screams just like a Barbie, and pulls my hair with beast paws.

We fight, kick, and scratch, shadowy beast and beautiful she-wolf. As we rumble down the stairs, the moon glass rises up in the air and hovers above us. We tumble down the hall, down the big marble steps, out the door . . .

. . . and onto the crowded front lawn.

The whole party erupts into chaos as we shoot

like a double arrow across the crowds. The Andra-beast and I separate for a moment. Then she takes off, and I chase her. I tackle her and we roll around on the grass. She bites my ankle, and I dig my nails into her back. She knocks me to the ground.

When I bolt up again, ready to fight on, I see three weregirls—Arielle, Nikki, and Grazia—leaping over the crowds, in full transformation. They catch up as we fight back across the abandoned garden. We all leap back toward the front lawn, and I don't know how we get past another set of gates—we're now fighting in the street outside. Some cache of firecrackers to be used at some final stage of the party catches fire; huffing and out of breath, with the firecrackers flickering on our faces, the four of us corner the Andra creature. The moon glass hovers above us in protection. But the Andra creature laughs a garbled laugh, like she knows something we don't.

"Like to like," she growls through her fangs.

"Yeah, I got it," I growl back, stepping toward her slowly, motioning Arielle, Grazia, and Nikki to surround her.

The Andra beast jumps on me. She pins me to the ground, blows her breath in my face.

I scream, knock her off me, against a tree. But

she has nine lives. She's back up in a blink.

"Sorry, Lily," she screams, "but this Earth's not big enough for both of us! Now it's *our time*! Like to like!" She growls the spell at everything: at the lawn in front of her house, still loaded with stupefied kids, at the mansion beyond, at the trees— and every shadow, every dark spot everywhere turns into a hideous beast. Even the roof of the house changes into a creature that's so long and scaly and reptilian—the slates of the roofing are its scales. The whole roof rolls down, breaks up into smaller reptiles, and quivers everywhere among the panicked guests. In a blink, the Breed surround us, snarling their fangs; their shapes and faces are so many, they're hideous yet wondrous, like toy monsters.

Andra lets out a roar, and the gang attacks us.

We turn and run. We're fast.

Behind us, the crowd spills out of the mansion's gate. Kids and catering people run furiously to their cars.

I peek back and see Josh's Cherokee stuck in a gridlock of scared partiers trying to drive away. The cars honk in counterpoint to our howls.

Then, leaving the cars behind, the bodies of the Breed slither and slink after us . . . chasing us. . . .

I look at the weregirls, and we're all like one body: we all leap and dive into the night, howling and shrieking.

Run! my father commands. *Run!*

But we don't want to give up as yet; we want to know our mettle. Like one body, we careen down a street I've never seen before, all made up of big gates and private driveways—and we turn, ready to fight. We bite, are bitten; we chase and are chased. A wild fight, back and forth, forcing the fleeing cars to back up, smashing into each other. Until the street clears of cars, becoming a plain battleground. Bodies onto bodies . . . Hair, teeth, and claws . . . We knock down one beast after another, but they're back on top of us faster than they fall. They close in, but then we race away with perfect speed. The faster we race, the more we feel our power.

Just ride, my father whispers. *You're faster than them!*

Even so harried, even bristling on every inch of my body, I manage to think, Dad's been keeping this from me. The Breed is fierce, but not that fierce! We can handle them!

I'm at the head of the pack, and when I look back—now I know what "weregirls riding" means!

Toes barely touching the streets. Flying. Heavenly pack! Otherworldly beautiful! *Dad, make the ride last!*

He must have heard me, because suddenly, turning a corner or leaping around a building, we get far ahead, or the Breed backs off, I'm not sure. When I look, they're no longer behind us.

The streets open ahead of us surreally.

The moon bounces onto the street, smearing everything in its milky light.

It bounces on ahead, until it guides us to my house, until . . .

. . . we crash into the half-finished swimming pool in my backyard, so humble compared to Andra's bedroom fountain.

The moon bounces on the trampled grass of the yard, then lifts, dizzily finding its way back into the sky, and from unseen heights, my dad grumbles, *You didn't listen to me. Reckless, irresponsible, and now soaked . . .*

We jump up in the cold water and climb out into the backyard—with just the moonlight on us. We look at each other's bodies just long enough to giggle. We're naked and glistening wet in moonlight. Racing into the house to rummage for dry towels, as if that humble doorstep in the back door of the kitchen was the frontier of magic . . .

. . . we're back in our girl bodies, the ones we know, yet now so magical. Arielle's the first to speak. "What happened back there?"

So this is what waking from a spell is like. With wet stringy hair, scratches on our faces, taste of skirmish and blood still on our lips. All that was ugly and scary was also exciting. Like to like! Link to link! The Breed! If Andra's claimed as a portal for the Breed because she yearns for dark power, so be it.

I think to Dad, *You can't protect me from dark power, as you can't protect me from growing up. I want my power, and I'll fight for it.*

I feel feverish, excited, and my hair's tangled beyond belief.

We raid my closet again, for dry clothes. Just as Nikki, still wet, slips into a T-shirt and jeans discolored from being laundered over and over, she screams, "Hey! My new dress. It's still at the mansion. Andra has my dress!"

"My God, our clothes are back there, that's a like-to-like problem," says Grazia so seriously I laugh out loud.

"But I don't want my mom to know," Grazia cries out.

She got Arielle panicked too. "The student body cards were in our clothes—she's got our pictures! Ask your dad, what's she gonna do now?"

"I don't care what she'll do—we'll deal it right back to her!"

I'm not frightened at all. I look around for the moon glass and I see it, lowering itself down onto the kitchen table.

"Good, we got protection," I say. "Now let's get some old movie and popcorn. Let's look like we had our own party."

We all chuckle. We feel whole—I can tell by the way we smile at one another. The moon glass is on the kitchen table. It looks like a regular little mirror. Then Arielle screams again. "Our cell phones! Our cell phones are at Andra's with our clothes! What's she going to do with our cells?"

"My mom's been wanting to cancel mine," says Grazia.

"Oh my God, no!" Arielle hollers. "I'm dead

without my cell. You gotta talk to your dad about that, Lily!"

I jump: the house phone is ringing. I race to pick it up.

First I can't understand the noise it's making. Someone's clearing his throat. Then I guess. "Josh . . ."

He sounds like he can hardly talk. "You back at your place?"

"Yeah, I'm here, with the girls. Where are you?"

"I'm actually still driving back. . . . The police stopped all the cars driving from that estate, and identified everyone. They booked a few kids who were drunk. It took forever. . . ."

"You all right, Josh?"

He recovers a little. "Yeah, a little dazed, I guess. . . . Lily, what was all that?" Then: "Wait, I don't want an explanation."

"Good. I'm not going to give you one."

"Lily?"

"Yeah?"

"Your mom was married to your dad, like, how many years?"

"Eleven years, and she survived."

He's quiet. I can't guess what he thinks. Did I

turn him off forever? But he says, rather gently, "So, magic really works for you."

"It did tonight." I wait. I can hear him breathe quietly—he's got the cell right near his lips. "Good night, Josh." Arielle starts gesturing wildly: *What are you doing, you hanging up?* But I'm hanging up. Let him sort this out and make up his own mind.

When I hear Mom pull up the driveway, it's close to dawn.

Mom unlocks the front door. When she sees us crashed on the couch and on the floor, she lets out a sigh that I hear from where I lie almost asleep. But she doesn't speak yet. She closes the door, then takes off her belt and holster, ammo pouches and handcuffs. By that time, I've pulled myself up. When we face each other, we smile, like we don't know what else to do. And then she says, "The department busted a party at the Hewlit mansion. There was some kind of fight. I heard that a gang showed up, and there were gunshots."

"Really," I say. "That's crazy, Mom. Who told you?"

"Tim told me. He got a call and drove over. When he got to the house everyone was running from it already. Most of the kids were from your school. I was convinced you'd be there."

I shake my head with all the conviction I can muster. *Who, me? That's not my setup, Mom! Nah!*

She walks over, sits next to me on the couch, hugs me like she hasn't done in a long while. "Tim called me for backup but I couldn't make it. I was on the other side of downtown. When I heard of kids running and screaming, I sort of freaked."

"I'm totally safe, Mom," I say. "Dad's protecting me."

"Enough of that, Lily. Please."

I smile. I think about telling Mom more, but she wouldn't be able to hear it—she's such an unmagical mom, she'll get all concerned and never get off my case. Then I think, but she'll have to get used to it, so I might tell her just a little bit, and then more some other time, and then gradually . . .

Meanwhile, I look back at my mom until the look of stress on her face begins to soften.

"Don't worry, Mom. I just wanted to say, Dad's here. I mean, I can't forget Dad, and I don't want to either, so, he's like . . . here all the time. You know what I mean?"

She answers, slowly. "Yeah, I know. All the time, and everywhere."

Then I get a throb in my heart, and I wonder. Flat though she is, what's Mom talking about? Memories only?

I don't want to ask any more questions. It's perfect, the way she said it.

So I say, "It's all right, Mom. I was just being metaphorical."

EPILOGUE
Andra

I bet they'll be talking about this party forever. I wish I had it on video. What was I thinking—I should have set up my web-cam to capture the look on Lily's face when she entered my room—priceless! But there's no rush. She and I will meet again.

The place is trashed. I'm lucky my parents are skiing in Switzerland. When I asked them to give me space for my celebration, Dad said fine. They wouldn't have stood for this—and I'm supposedly getting all my wishes, always.

I reach from where I lie in bed, turn on the intercom. I call Pilar, our Guatemalan house-keeper. The one woman in this house who knows everything about me—the way servants do. They're worse than mothers, but also better—you can fire them. We've had her for years. Dad had fake papers made for her and her family. She had her own kids between sixteen and twenty-two, when she started working for us. Finished motherhood when my mother hadn't even started. "You there, Pilar?"

Means "pillar," in Spanish. Of faith, or something. I guess, she *is* the pillar of this house.

"*Buenos días,* Miss Andra."

"Morning. Get everyone together and clean the house."

"Nobody's here."

"I don't care. Get some people to clean up this mess. Call your cousins from Guatemala or something."

"Sure, Miss Andra."

She doesn't lose her temper. Everyone else here does. At me, of course. I do my best to set them off. I can't set off Pilar, don't know why. Mystery. I don't have the time right now. I ring another room. "Holden?"

He doesn't answer.

"Hol-DEN!"

"Yeah, yeah." Groggily. "Do you have to yell?"

"You're still sleeping! Wake up, I need you."

"Not again."

"Yes, again! Payback. You lost the video of Lily's house. Get up and help clean the mess."

I throw off my silk sheets, land on the brand-new floor, walk on sweaty feet, *fwakk, fwakk.* I hear my footfalls, I hear *everything.* My senses are still so sharpened from last night. I lunge to the fountain to look into the water.

There they are, my new kin. Floating in aquatic slumber. I breathe in relief. They haven't vanished with the fogs of dawn.

As recently as several days ago, before the game against Lily's scraggly gang, this was all a fantasy. Not anymore! I kneel over the fountain, and let my reflection mingle in—still me, blond, beautiful, and juiced with new power. Then my reflection begins to change. I love that the change starts with my eyes. They become slits—*different.*

I always knew I was different. My "legal" *papa* and *maman* had three boys before they realized they weren't going to have a daughter. If I call them my "legals," I don't have to say "parents," a word I really hate.

Anyway, *maman,* who loathed childbirth, still wanted to try to have a girl. When she knew they couldn't have one, they adopted me. So of course they never felt like my family. Now I stare at those swirling contours below the surface of the water, querying them in thought: *Are you going to feel like my real family? Connected, close, more comfortable even than my favorite clothes? I want you as my family!*

Then I see Lily, in the fountain. I see her talking to me last night, then trying to turn off the waters and stop the Breed. She tried to warn me. The poor can be so sweet. I really like her—but what was that crap she was trying to sell me? I have a choice? Of course I have a choice. That's the most thrilling part of this, that I'm making the best choice for myself: intimacy in evil—that's hot!

I tickle the water. The images change. I see Lily score her breakaway goal in our game. I knew as soon as she broke free from our defense that she wasn't running by herself. No normal human could run that fast. That's when I felt it: major hate for this normal girl (well, not so normal, really), almost like the hate I have for my absentee parents—who are they, where are they? And who is me, really? What am I really like? I guess this is the best way to find out, so exciting, like signing up for an incredibly weird chat room, and then planning to meet these people you don't even know. Then you get the shocks delivered, in real life. Only question left is: How will I measure up? I can't wait to find out!

I stare intently in the water, but I get no image of Lily beaten and crestfallen. Maybe this water doesn't project the future, or maybe it won't be that easy, Lily's tough—after our rumble last night, I'm pretty sore. Aaahh, when I stole the moon glass out of her house, I should've rummaged and gotten her log too, but I was too nervous. It's all right; I got time. I had one taste of her blood last night. She had one of mine too. This is the bummer, that I can't ask *her,* "What was it like for you? Let's compare!"

As I stare into the fountain, the image changes. I see that boy. Josh. Can I use *him* to ambush Lily? And then, I hear this voice, commanding and yet so smooth.

Josh is a flat, he says. *He won't be much use to you.*

You don't know that, I counter. *And why aren't you showing yourself?*

Because you're being tested. And you're talking back to me already.

That's my style. I grin into the water, but then,

as I can't see the Breed Master in it, I turn to stare at my endless bedroom.

I still don't see him.

Sit, he growls, so threatening, I freak. *Sit and listen! You can't use that boy.*

Is he telling the truth? Is this magic thing starting with not getting the guy you're in the mood for? That can't be. He's just powering me!

Flats are too tricky. They jam magical connections.

I think, He's full of it. I'm around flats all the time. My adoptive dad is a flat par excellence. So is my adoptive mom—and they never made me feel that I wasn't made for this! Never mind. I'll play it cool. I'll pierce through this. I stamp my feet on the floor, feeling dust under my heels and toes. I'll kill Pilar, she's getting way too comfy in this job!

Where are you going? he asks.

I didn't know I needed permission to move around, I say, and suddenly, I skid, and fall, and land on my butt. OW!

You're going to sit still now?

I suddenly decide, all right, I'm in this, I'll play by its rules—for now.

Get up, he says, in that low, smooth, all-power

voice. *Go to your desk, grab a pen, and start writing this down. Lesson one: No improvising. We can't take another chance on your improvising. Spells are an exact science. There is so much more you need to know. . . .*

End of *Weregirls: Birth of the Pack*

ACKNOWLEDGMENTS

I had wanted to write in the young adult genre for many years, but felt intimidated by how demanding young readers really are. They won't tolerate self-indulgent writing, they want books that are simple and yet not shallow, they want them visual without being cartoonlike, and they hate writing that tries too hard. It was a wonderful challenge. I was helped by my sophisticated editor, Susan Chang, who guided me with a delicate touch and made the editing process fascinating. My daughter, Chloe, who is the real heroine of this story, was my other great help. Valuable insights and comments came from Mary Hanlon Stone, Carl Dallabadia, Caldecot Chubb (the most literate movie producer I ever met), John Silbersack, Adam Popescu, Iris Popescu, and from the now so missed Janice Garber. I thank them all again.